"Sold, to the gentleman in the back row."

Lacey looked out into the crowd at the person holding the numbered paddle. Squinting against the sunlight, she glanced over the man's square jaw and deep-set dark eyes. The cowboy hat shaded a lot of his face, but there was no mistaking who he was. Her heart raced as she followed his movement through the crowd, closely examining the man she'd remembered from so many years ago. Her gaze moved over his long torso to those broad shoulders.

He might have looked military, but there was a lot of Texas cowboy mixed in. Tall and muscular, he filled out a shirt like no other man she'd seen in a long time.

He glanced over his shoulder. Their eyes met for a second, and Lacey felt that odd feeling, a mixture of longing, sadness and a bit of anger. Before she could move or even acknowledge him, he turned and walked away.

So Master Sergeant Jeff Gentry had finally come home.

Harlequin® Romance brings you

PATRICIA THAYER's

Home to Texas and straight to the altar!

A home. A family. A legacy of their own.

Mustang Valley has long been home to the brotherhood. United by blood, trust and loyalty, these men fight for what they believe—for family, for what's right and ultimately…for love.

Now it's time. Time for the next generation!

The Lionhearted Cowboy Returns

Hearts are fluttering because Jeff Gentry's back and about to cause a whole heap of trouble!

PATRICIA THAYER

The Lionhearted Cowboy Returns

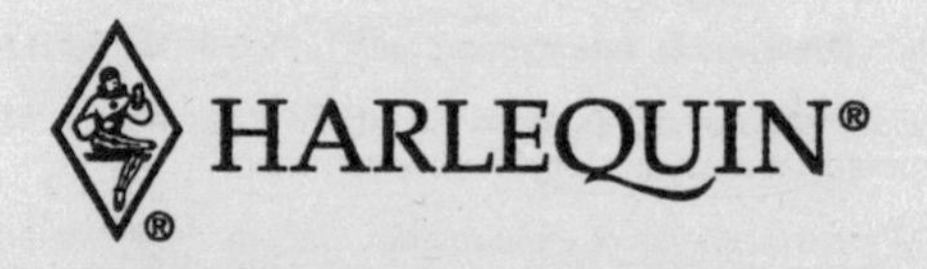

TORONTO • NEW YORK • LONDON
AMSTERDAM • PARIS • SYDNEY • HAMBURG
STOCKHOLM • ATHENS • TOKYO • MILAN • MADRID
PRAGUE • WARSAW • BUDAPEST • AUCKLAND

ISBN-13: 978-0-373-17661-8

THE LIONHEARTED COWBOY RETURNS

First North American Publication 2010.

This edition published by arrangement with Harlequin Books S.A.

For questions and comments about the quality of this book please contact us at Customer_eCare@Harlequin.ca.

www.eHarlequin.com

Printed in U.S.A.

Originally born and raised in Muncie, Indiana, **Patricia Thayer** is the second of eight children. She attended Ball State University, and soon afterwards headed West. Over the years she's made frequent visits back to the Midwest, trying to keep up with her growing family.

Patricia has called Orange County, California, home for many years. She not only enjoys the warm climate, but also the company and support of other published authors in the local writers' organization. For the past eighteen years she has had the unwavering support and encouragement of her critique group. It's a sisterhood like no other.

When not working on a story, you might find her traveling the United States and Europe, taking in the scenery and doing story research while thoroughly enjoying herself accompanied by Steve, her husband for over thirty-five years. Together they have three grown sons and four grandsons. As she calls them, her own true-life heroes. On rare days off from writing, you might catch her at Disneyland, spoiling those grandkids rotten! She also volunteers for the Grandparent Autism Network.

Patricia has written for over twenty years and has authored more than thirty-five books for Harlequin. She has been nominated for both a National Readers' Choice Award and a prestigious RITA® Award. Her book *Nothing Short of a Miracle* won an *RT Book Reviews* Reviewers' Choice award.

A longtime member of Romance Writers of America, she has served as president and held many other board positions for her local chapter in Orange County. She's a firm believer in giving back.

Check her Web site at www.patriciathayer.com for upcoming books.

To all the men and women in our armed forces;
Thank you for your service to our country.
And to my Tom in the U.S. Army,
you make a mother proud. Stay safe and God speed.

CHAPTER ONE

HE'D been to hell and back, but he'd finally made it... home.

Jeff Gentry stood on the porch of the foreman's cottage at the Rocking R Ranch. The sun was just coming up, but he was already feeling the Texas summer heat. He drew a long breath of the familiar country air, loving the earthy smells of cattle and horses. This place was where he'd grown up, where he'd been part of a family. As a kid, it was the first place he'd ever felt safe.

This had been the meaning of home to him, once. Could it be again?

For the past decade, the U.S. Army had been his home. Ten years was a long time. During his military service, he'd traveled the world and seen far too much destruction and death to resemble the kid who'd left the ranch at twenty. Now he had his own personal nightmares he needed to forget. And he lived with a particular one that had changed his life for good. He rubbed his thigh, still feeling pain. But, like the doctor had told him, he'd been one of the lucky ones.

He didn't feel so lucky. The last mission had robbed

him of his life as he'd known it, and of his future. And now he'd been sent home to figure out his next move. Could he come back to San Angelo and rejoin the Randell family?

"Morning, son."

Jeff turned to see his father approach the porch. He put on a smile. "Hey, Dad."

At fifty-five years old, Wyatt Gentry-Randell was still a formidable man. He walked tall, his spine straight. His muscular frame resulted from years of physical labor handling rodeo stock. He smiled easily, and he was a soft touch when it came to his wife and children.

Years ago, he'd married Maura Wells and taken on her two small children, Jeff and Kelly. The day Wyatt had adopted them had been the best day of Jeff's life. Wyatt had erased a lot of years of painful memories for their mother, for all of them. And two more siblings, Andrew and Rachel, had been added into the mix.

Oh, yeah, he loved this man.

"What brings you out here?" Jeff asked, knowing that most of the family had given him what he'd asked for: space. "Do you need my help with anything?"

Wyatt handed him a mug filled with steaming coffee. "No. I just wanted to spend some time with my son. It's nice to have you home."

Jeff took a sip. "It's good to be back." It wasn't a lie exactly. He enjoyed being here with his parents.

He leaned against the porch railing and looked around the impressive ranch. Every well-cared-for outbuilding had recently been painted glossy white. For over twenty years, twin brothers Wyatt and Dylan had run their rough-stock business here. Not only did Uncle

Dylan raise Brahmas, he had a bull-riding school, too. Both were very profitable enterprises, and also came under the umbrella of the Randell Corporation, of which every family member was a paid shareholder.

The corporation had been formed about a dozen years ago by Wyatt and Dylan along with the other four Randell brothers, Chance, Cade, Travis and Jarred, plus two cousins, Luke and Brady. All their properties were involved, including a nature retreat and an authentic working cattle ranch. They'd also built horse-property homes in a gated community that overlooked the famous Mustang Valley where wild ponies roamed freely. That was a big tourist draw.

Even though Jeff and his sister weren't blood, they'd always been considered Randells. And he had no doubt that the family would find a place even for a beat-up old soldier like him in the organization. But that was what he didn't want—pity.

His father's voice broke into his reverie. "We know the last several months have been rough, son. So take all the time you need. Just get used to being home again."

It was hard to hang on to anger when you had that kind of support. Jeff was touched, but he wasn't ready to talk about his time overseas, maybe not for a long time. If ever. He'd done enough of that after his rescue, during his months of rehab, and it hadn't done a bit of good.

"I appreciate that, but I'm fine." He forced that smile again. "Of course, I should take advantage of this to get out of work. I've never been fond of mucking out stalls."

His father grinned. "It's safe to say we have enough

ranch hands to do that task. But maybe you're up to going for a ride with Hank and I this morning?"

Jeff tensed. He wasn't ready to meet up with all the Randell clan. "Where to?"

Wyatt sighed. "A ranch auction." He studied his son. "The Guthrie place."

Jeff couldn't hide his shock at the mention of his childhood friend. "Trevor was having financial trouble?" he managed to ask, knowing it was a crazy question. After his friend's death Lacey would have trouble handling things by herself.

Lacey Haynes Guthrie. Just hearing her name sent a rush through him. Damn, he hated that she still had that effect on him. In school, she was the girl everyone loved, but she'd only had eyes for one man and that was his best friend. Never him—until that one day.

"Why didn't anyone say something sooner?"

His father looked at him. "First, you and your recovery were our main concern. And secondly, we didn't know there were problems until I heard about the auction this morning." He blew out a long breath. "With this economy, so many ranches are in trouble. And Trevor's illness was costly..." His father raised an eyebrow. "Maybe you can talk with Lacey today."

For years Jeff had tried never to think about her. It seemed like a lifetime ago when they'd all been friends. Best friends. Now Trevor was gone. "I don't know what to say." He released a breath. "How can I explain why I wasn't around?"

"You tell her the truth, son. You were defending our country, and there was your extended stay in the hospital. All those surgeries on your leg. You've gone through a lot. There's no shame in what happened to you."

Jeff closed his eyes, trying to push aside the pain of the past year. "Dad, Lacey doesn't need to hear my problems. She's had enough to deal with." He glanced at his father. "And it's not something I'm ready to talk about yet."

Wyatt nodded. "Okay, we'll honor your decision. But I still think you should get out today." A truck pulled up to the house. "Come on, your granddad's here. And knowing your mom, she's cooked up a storm. If you don't show up, she gives your food to me." He rubbed his flat stomach. "I've already had to loosen my belt a notch."

He hated to worry his parents. "Okay, I'll save you from blueberry-pancake overload."

Jeff smiled and it felt good. His dad kept his pace slow as they walked up toward the house. Breakfast with his parents and Hank would be the easy part. The hard part would be later, seeing Lacey again, knowing he couldn't say or do anything that would ease her loss. Or the fact he hadn't been there for his friend.

Jeff could never forgive himself for that.

Later that morning, Lacey Guthrie walked away when handlers led out her deceased husband's best pair of quarter horses. The coal-black stallion, Rebel Run, and the pretty liver-chestnut filly, Doc's Fancy Girl, were supposed to have been Trevor's best breeding stock. If they were sold off, there was no way she could keep the business going. But today's auction was about survival first.

"Next up for bidding are numbers 107 and 108 in your programs," the auctioneer began. "Anyone from this area knows the bloodlines of these two fine animals. We'll start the bidding on Rebel…"

Fighting tears, Lacey stepped into her kitchen, shut the back door, and leaned her head against the glass pane. She couldn't watch them go. They represented the last of her dreams with Trevor. Their quarter horse ranch. What they'd worked so hard on for the past ten years was never going to come true. What about Colin and Emily?

"Oh, Trevor," she sobbed. "You should be here for us."

"Mom!"

Lacey quickly wiped away the tears and put a smile on her face as she turned around to her eight-year-old son. "What is it, Colin?"

"You can't sell Rebel and Fancy," he said, his fists clenched. "They're Dad's horses."

"We've talked about this, son. I don't have a choice." She went to him and reached out to brush his shaggy blond hair from his forehead. He jerked away.

"Yes, you do," he insisted. "Go out there and stop it. Dad doesn't want you to sell 'em."

"Dad isn't here, honey. And I'm doing what I have to do to keep our ranch," she told him, knowing her words weren't going to make any difference.

Anger flashed in the boy's eyes, eyes a deep blue so much like his father's. "You didn't love Dad. If you did you wouldn't do this." He turned and ran out, the screen door banging against the porch wall before slamming shut.

Lacey started after him and got to the porch just in time to hear the auctioneer's gavel hit the table as he shouted, "Sold, to the gentleman in the back row."

Lacey looked out into the crowd at the person holding the numbered paddle. Squinting against the sunlight, she glanced over the man's square jaw and the deep-set dark eyes. The cowboy hat shaded most of his face, but there was no mistaking who he was. Her heart raced as she followed his movement through the crowd, closely examining the man she'd remembered from so many years ago. Her gaze moved over his long torso to those broad shoulders.

He might have looked military, but there was a lot of Texas cowboy mixed in. Tall and muscular, he filled out a shirt like no other man she'd seen in a long time.

He glanced over his shoulder. Their eyes met for a second, and Lacey felt that odd feeling, a mixture of longing, sadness and a little anger. Before she could move or even acknowledge him, he turned and walked away.

So, Master Sergeant Jeff Gentry had finally come home.

Jeff couldn't believe it. He didn't even know about his own future, but he owned two horses. He'd only planned to bid to help Lacey get top dollar for them. He couldn't let her lose everything. This ranch had been Trevor's dream for his family. He knew his friend had worked hard to build a reputation.

His father caught up to him. "Do you mind my asking what you plan to do with your quarter horses?"

Jeff shrugged. "Sorry, I guess I didn't think about where I could board them."

Wyatt smiled. "Of course you can bring them to the ranch or maybe take them over to Uncle Chance's place. He's better equipped for training anyway."

Hank walked over to them. Jeff's eighty-five-year-old grandfather was grinning. Still healthy and active, Hank Barrett was the head of the Randell family.

"I'd say you got yourself a fine pair of horses, Jeff." He glanced around. "I'm surprised Chance didn't show up this morning. He's always been impressed with Trevor's stock."

Jeff looked toward the house again. Lacey Guthrie was still on the porch. His breath caught as his hungry gaze moved over her. Tall and slender, she was nearly five foot nine. Her long legs were encased in faded jeans. She'd filled out since high school, and the weight looked good on her. Really good. Her honey-blond hair was thick and silky, hanging to her shoulders in soft waves. Her eyes were grass-green. He remembered her as always smiling, but she was not today. Definitely not the last time he'd seen her, either.

"Do you want to go talk with Lacey?" his dad asked.

Jeff shook his head. "She's busy right now." He pulled his attention away from her. "I'd better go pay for the horses and make arrangement for pick-up." Before his dad or granddad could say anything more, he walked off, unable to hide the limp. He fought the discomfort and pulled out his checkbook as he headed to the cashier. The cost was high, but not nearly what he owed his friend.

Later, Jeff shifted his dad's pickup into four-wheel drive and turned off the gravel road. The oversized tires made the journey easily over the rough terrain along the pathway to the clearing. His spirits began to soar when the familiar lineman's shack came into view. He stopped the truck and climbed out, but didn't go any further as his gaze took in the landscape, the grove of trees and the stream that ran through the Guthrie property.

Hundreds of happy memories of summer days he'd spent here with his friend came rushing back. As kids, he and Trevor would ride their horses up here, wade through the stream, even pretend to fight off villains, rustlers and any bad guy on the most-wanted list. They ran races through the field to see who would win the title that summer as the fastest kid.

Jeff had always won. He was the athletic one. Trevor was the outgoing one, the charmer with animals and people. When it came to girls, Trev had led the way, too. That was how his friend had won Lacey's heart.

He turned his attention to the shack. Their hangout. It was different now. What once was nearly falling down had been rebuilt. Trevor had written saying what he'd planned to do.

Jeff walked across the new porch floor. The door had new hinges, too. Trying the knob, he discovered it was unlocked. Although the inside was dim, there was light coming through the windows.

"Looks like you did it, Trev," he whispered into the single-room cabin. "You fixed the place up."

Suddenly the emotions were overwhelming. He drew a few breaths and released them slowly as a doctor had once instructed him. Once he'd pulled himself together again, he began to look around.

A small table and a pair of chairs were placed against one wall, on the other were built-in bunk beds. In the corner was a pot-bellied stove. He walked to the kitchen area to find the same old brass water pump arching over the oversized sink.

He touched the aged counter, tracing the familiar initials scratched in the wood. Their names, *Trevor*

Guthrie, Jeff Gentry, and then, later, another person had been invited into their sanctum, Lacey Haynes.

When they'd gone to high school, a new declaration had been carved out: *Trevor loves Lacey.* Jeff's finger outlined the heart around their names. The threesome turned into a twosome. Trevor and Lacey never intentionally left him out, but he'd become the third wheel. And he'd found it harder and harder to be around the happy couple. Even dating his own steady girl hadn't changed his feelings for Lacey. But she'd loved Trevor.

Jeff had tried to accept it. After a time, he knew he couldn't stay around. He'd joined the military and was to leave in a few months. It had been a rough summer for all of them, and particularly rocky for the perfect couple. Trevor had asked him to help. Jeff had reluctantly agreed and he'd met Lacey at the cabin. But they hadn't done much talking.

Jeff drew a shaky breath; the pain and joy of being with Lacey still tore at him.

He'd done the unforgivable that day. He'd betrayed his best friend. So the only thing he could do had been to leave and try to forget. He'd heard weeks later of the couple's wedding.

So many years had gone by. So many things had happened over those years. He rubbed his thigh absently.

"What are you doing here?"

Jeff spun around, nearly losing his balance. He gripped the counter as he looked at the young boy standing in the doorway. The kid's hat was cocked low, but there was no hiding his anger. There was no doubt at all that he was Trevor's son.

"Hi, I'm Jeff Gentry. I used to come here when I was a kid."

"This cabin belongs to me and my dad. So you've got to leave."

"I knew your dad, Trevor." He nodded. "You must be Colin."

The boy ignored him. "He's dead."

"I know and I'm sorry. I've been away for a lot of years."

Colin's eyes narrowed. "Dad told me you were in the army, Special Forces. That you're a hero."

Jeff tried not to flinch at the title. "I was just doing my job."

Those questioning blue eyes studied him. "Big deal. If you were my dad's friend, how come you never came to see him?"

"I was out of the country, serving overseas. As much as I wanted to be here, I had a job to do for the government."

The kid remained silent.

Jeff continued in the awkward stillness. "We wrote back and forth." That sounded lame, even to him. "I had no idea he was so sick until afterwards. I'm here now, so if I can help you—"

The kid reared back. "I don't need your help. 'Cause it's too late." Fighting tears, he ran out of the cabin.

"Wait, Colin." Jeff started after him, but stopped as he spotted a battered Jeep pull up next to his truck. Lacey Guthrie got out and walked up to her son. She didn't look happy with him.

Finally the boy stalked off toward the horse grazing on the grass. The eight-year-old mounted the animal with the ease of a pro, grabbed the reins and reeled him around. Feeling Colin's kick against his ribs, the horse shot off.

* * *

Lacey closed her eyes and prayed for strength, then she turned around to deal with the intruder at the cabin door.

Why wasn't she surprised to find Jeff here? So he wanted to reminisce about the past. Too bad he hadn't gotten the urge sooner. The one thing Trevor had wanted during those last days was to see his friend. As far as she was concerned she'd never wanted to see him again. She blinked away the sudden rush of tears. Why did he have to come back now?

She drew a shuddering breath and worked up the courage to speak. "So, Gentry, you finally made it home."

He stepped off the porch and made his way across the field. His movement was slow and uneven as he finally reached her. "I got here as soon as I could."

She nodded, not wanting to hear another condolence for her loss. "Your parents explained you were out of the country."

He cocked his head and held her gaze. His strong jaw showed a trace of his stubbornness, but his brown eyes gave away his softer side.

And his sexy side. Jeff Gentry had always been the quiet, sexy type. He still was.

"You have to know, Lacey, I'd have given anything to be here for Trevor."

She wasn't going to cry. "I know, but I'm not happy about your trick this morning."

"Trick?"

"You could at least have let me know you were back."

"Yeah, I should have. I've been staying pretty close to home."

The Jeff she remembered never gave much away.

Now wasn't much different. "I don't need your help now, Jeff. I don't need you to come and rescue me."

"Who said I was rescuing you?"

She folded her arms across her chest. "You're in the military, Master Sergeant. What do you need with quarter horses?"

"My time's up. I'm a civilian now."

She couldn't hide her shock. "I can't believe it."

He glanced away, but she caught a flash of sadness. "Believe it. I've given my time to my country. I'm ready for a change."

She could see the strain around his eyes. She had a feeling war had taken its toll on him. "Trevor would have loved having you back home."

He looked hesitant. "He wasn't the only one, Lace."

She hated that he called her by her nickname. "Logically, I know that..."

He nodded. "Trevor understood I had a job to do."

She turned and marched to her vehicle. The hurt she felt seemed as intense as losing Trevor all over again. Her biggest problems were that she had to deal with her husband being gone—and Jeff Gentry returning.

CHAPTER TWO

A few hours later, Jeff drove to the Guthrie Ranch. He wasn't going to leave things unsettled. Lacey might not want him around, but too bad, he didn't like the situation any more than she did.

Whether she liked it or not, he was back.

He pulled up in front of the house that had once been Trevor's parents' home.

He'd been here numerous times as a kid. Just as Trevor had been a frequent visitor at the Rocking R.

He went straight to the back porch and knocked on the door. It opened, and behind the screen a little girl about five years old appeared, wearing jeans and a pink-flowered blouse. He was caught off guard for a moment. She favored her mother with that same streaked blond hair and big eyes. The fight inside him suddenly died.

"Who are you?" the child asked.

"Jeff Gentry." He smiled. "I'm a friend of your mom and dad. Who are you?"

"Emily Susan Guthrie." She shook her head. "You can't see my daddy, he died."

Jeff leaned down, bracing his hands on his thighs. "I know, and I'm sorry, Emily."

She seemed to brighten a little. "My daddy used to call me Emmy Sue," she announced proudly.

"That's cute. Is your mother here?"

"She's down at the barn, feeding the horses. I have to stay here and watch TV. She only lets Colin help her 'cause he's older."

"I bet when you're older, she'll let you help, too."

"I used to help my daddy. He said I was his best girl."

Jeff could still remember years ago how Wyatt used to call his younger sister Kelly 'Princess.' "I bet you were. And I bet your daddy would be happy that you're minding your mom, too."

She nodded eagerly. "And I'm not s'posed to let anybody in the house when she's not here."

At least one of this family's members was talking to him. "That's a good thing. I'll just go down to the barn and see your mother there."

The child looked disappointed. "'Kay. Bye." She shut the door.

Jeff made his way down the steps, wishing he could spend the afternoon watching television, too. Instead he had to try and think of what to say to Lacey to convince her to accept some help.

He owed Trevor that much.

"Mom, I'm finished feeding the horses," Colin called as he came out of Fancy's stall. "Am I done now?"

Lacey looked around the nearly empty horse barn. Thanks to the successful auction that morning, there were only five horses left, and two more would soon be gone.

She pointed to the leather bridles tossed over the

railing. "Just take those back to the tack room and you can go to the house, but I don't want you to bother your sister."

Her son grabbed the tack off the railing and started down the center aisle. "You always blame me for all the trouble."

"That's because you can't leave Emily alone. I mean it, Colin, don't go near her. You're already in trouble for riding off today without asking."

"Fine, I'll just go to my room." He went into the tack room, then came out seconds later. She knew he hadn't had time to put away the bridles properly, but it wasn't worth the argument; she'd just do it herself later.

It had been a long day and she was tired. The auction had taken a lot out of her. At least the money made today would finally pay off Trevor's medical bills, and the ranch would be solvent for the next year. After that, she wasn't sure what she'd do. She knew she couldn't continue the breeding business without a stud. She'd kept her chestnut broodmare, Bonnie. She just needed a stallion.

She looked toward the barn door where her son had stopped to talk with someone. Jeff Gentry. Great. She didn't need any more of him today, but by the looks of it, she wasn't going to get her wish.

She watched as he started down the aisle. Large and powerfully built from years of military life, he roamed efficiently. Her gaze moved over him and noticed a slow gait and a slight limp. Had he been hurt? She hadn't heard anything about any injuries.

He made a stop at Reb's stall and began to get acquainted with the stallion. Much like Trevor, Jeff had a knack with animals, maybe more so than with people.

It had surprised her and everyone else when he'd announced that he'd joined the military. Even though college hadn't worked out for him, she'd always thought he'd partner with his dad and uncle in the rough-stock business. His decision to go into the army had affected a lot of people, including her. She had a feeling his return would affect just as many.

No, she couldn't let it affect her. Not after all this time and after everything she'd gone through.

Jeff gave Reb's muzzle one more pat, then started toward her. A strange sensation surged through her and all she could do was watch him. He was a good-looking man, but so was Trevor, although the two friends couldn't have been more different. Trevor was blond with hazel eyes, while Jeff had dark-brown hair and brooding coffee-colored eyes.

She thought back, recalling their conversation earlier. How could she have talked to him that way? Even with the hurt and months of loneliness since Trevor's death, she had no right to blame Jeff. He hadn't caused the virus that had damaged her husband's heart. Yet she couldn't bring herself to apologize for her actions. They had too much history for that. Jeff hadn't only walked away from Trevor all those years ago, he'd walked away from her, too. With not even a care, or as much as a backward glance. Jeff Gentry never realized the pain and hurt he'd caused her. It had been Trevor who'd picked up the pieces.

Lacey drew a breath and released it. Now, ten years later, she knew it was finally time to let it go.

"I take it you're here for your horses."

Jeff paused to regroup for his talk with Lacey. He wasn't going to let her brush him off. He could do attitude with the best of 'em. "First, I want to settle something."

"Settle what?"

"Can we cut this out? I get you're angry at me for just showing up."

She threw him a surprised look. "Why don't we just chalk it up to a bad day?" Her gaze locked with his. "You ever felt your world was suddenly crashing down around you?"

Jeff gripped the stall railing, shifting his weight onto his good leg. "Hell, yes, once or twice," he answered, flashing back to the painful days during his long recovery.

He'd only heard of Trevor's illness right after surgery when he was flat on his back, fighting his own hell. His friend was dying and he couldn't help him. He'd sent word to Lacey, but by the looks of it, that hadn't been enough.

"Trevor wouldn't want you wasting time being so angry," he said.

Those pretty green eyes narrowed. "Cut me a little slack, Gentry. I had to give up a lot today."

"I'm not cutting you anything. You can't fall apart now. You have kids who need you."

She shot him a look. "Who are you to tell me what I need to do? You weren't here. It might not be reasonable to blame that on you, but he was your best friend."

He tried not to flinch. "The military doesn't care about friendships, Lace. And neither did the terrorists I was fighting. There were times I couldn't even contact my parents."

He closed his eyes for a moment as he took a breath. The last he'd heard from Trevor, he'd said everything was fine. That had been about a month before he'd been deployed on his last mission. Then everything had changed.

He shook away his wayward thoughts.

"Lacey, you've got to know, if it were humanly possible, I would have found a way to be here for him."

He couldn't take his eyes off her. She'd always been pretty, and that had only been enhanced with age. "For you, too."

"I didn't need your help, then or now," she said stubbornly.

"That's just too bad," he retorted.

She froze at his words, then snapped out of the daze. "Look around, Gentry, there isn't much left."

Jeff moved closer, feeling fatigue in every step. He ignored it. "That's why you need me."

She said something very unladylike, grabbed a feed pail and started down the aisle. Jeff reached for her arm and turned her around. "Tell me, Lacey. How bad are things?"

"That's none of your business." She started off again.

Jeff went after her, pushing hard to keep up. She went into the tack room.

"Is Rebel Run your only stud?"

Lacey busied herself hanging up the bridles. "As of this morning he's *your* stud."

So she didn't have any business left. Great. "Okay, here's the deal. I need a place to board my horses. I'd like to leave Rebel and Fancy here. I'll pay you a fair price."

She looked shocked. "You're kidding, right?"

"Since when have you known me to kid around?" He paused and waited for her answer, but got none.

"Okay, here's the clincher. I need a place to stay." He released a breath. "And I want to rent the cabin."

Lacey ran her sleeve over her brow, pushing her worn hat off her forehead. She threw up a silent prayer this day would end, along with all the craziness. She didn't want this man messing in her life.

Lacey looked back at Jeff. "The Randells own more property around here than anyone. You can take Rebel over to your uncle's place, put him out to stud there."

He gave a shrug. "I have my reasons. So, you want to take me up on my offer? The money couldn't hurt."

"All right, the horses can stay."

He nodded. "You should think about boarding other horses, too. Bring in another half dozen and you'd make a good income."

She shook her head. "I can't work at the market and handle more animals without help."

"Then hire someone," he said. "Until then, I'll come by and help out."

She jammed her hands on her hips. "If this is your trick way of rescuing me, I don't want it."

His dark gaze settled on her face. "It's the other way around, Lace. You're the one rescuing me."

The next morning about 6:00 a.m., Jeff walked in the back door of his parents' house and found his mother standing at the stove cooking breakfast. The aroma of coffee and bacon hit him.

Maura Gentry looked up and smiled. With her auburn hair and green eyes, she had always been pretty, and that hadn't changed over the ten years he'd been away. Even though she'd come to the Rocking R a city girl, she'd fitted into ranch life as if born to it.

"Morning, honey." She eyed him closely, unable to hide her concern.

"Hi, Mom. Something smells good." He walked to the table and pulled out a chair. The kitchen had always been the heart of this home. It had also been remodeled a few times. The cabinets were maple with dark granite countertops and the latest stainless-steel appliances. The floor was the original honey hardwood. He'd loved growing up in this house.

She set a plate on the table. "I made sweet rolls."

He picked one up and took a bite. "You keep this up and I'm going to gain ten pounds."

"You could use some extra weight."

He frowned and took another bite. After he swallowed, he asked, "Where's Dad?"

"He's with Dylan. The new bull arrived earlier. He should be here soon." She brought over a plate piled high with bacon. Just then the back door opened and his dad walked in. He hung his hat on the hook on the wall, then nodded to his son before he went to his wife and kissed her.

He came to the table and pulled out a chair. "Mornin', son."

"Morning, Dad."

"You've got to see this bull, Jeff. Dylan's named him Rough Ride." His father beamed. "We both think he's going to make quite a reputation on the circuit."

Maura Gentry brought a dish of scrambled eggs and joined them. "Just so long as the two of you stay away from him, I'm happy."

Wyatt frowned. "Are you saying I'm too old to climb on a bull?"

"No, I'm saying you're too smart. So don't make me

out a liar. Save the ride for those twenty-something kids who need to impress the girls." She picked up a fork. "You can impress me in other ways."

Jeff should have been used to his parents' flirting. Since the moment they'd met it had been like that between them.

His dad winked. "I'll do my best." He looked at his son. "You thought about what you're going to do with the horses?"

Jeff shrugged. "Only that I'm going to leave them at Lacey's and pay her to board them."

"So you've got no plans to go into the breeding business?" his dad asked.

Jeff scooped up a forkful of eggs. "Still thinking on that one. I need to find a place to live first."

His parents exchanged a look, then turned to him. His mother spoke. "You know you can stay in the cottage here as long as you want. There's no hurry to leave."

"I need to be closer to the Guthrie place. That's why I'm planning to move up to the cabin."

His dad swallowed his food. "What cabin?"

"The one where Trevor and I used to hang out."

His mother frowned. "That old lineman's shack? It was nearly falling down years ago."

Jeff took a drink of his orange juice. He understood his parents' concern. "Trevor must have put some work into it, because it's in good shape now."

His mother didn't look convinced. "Jeff, do you think it's a good idea to move so far away? It's pretty isolated there."

He'd been isolated in a lot worse places…the hills of Afghanistan, the deserts of Iraq. "Mom, it's only a few miles from the ranch house. Besides, I like the quiet."

"Haven't we left you alone?" she asked. "I only worry about you because of the…accident. You haven't been walking again that long." Her eyes filled with worry. "You've only been home ten days."

He didn't want to hurt either one of them. "I've had months of physical therapy. Yes, both of you have given me space while I've been here, and I appreciate it. But I'm too old to live at home. Mainly, I've got to come to grips with what I'm going to do with the rest of my life. I never dreamed it would be anything but the military. I hadn't planned to retire for another ten years."

This time his father spoke up. "I know you'd be happier in the army, son, I only wish that were an option."

Jeff shook his head. "Not if I can't do what I was trained for." And now that a terrorist sniper had changed everything for him, he had to make a different kind of life. "Right now, I need some time."

His mother started to talk, but his dad stopped her. "Maura, our son is a man. He needs to make his own decisions. Whatever that is, Jeff, we're proud of you."

The praise from Wyatt Gentry meant more to Jeff than any medal he'd received from that last mission.

Maura nodded. "I guess it's the best solution for you both. Lacey can use your help, too." His mother reached for his hand and smiled. "I think you can be a big help to each other."

The next day Hank Barrett drove up the road toward the cabin. He knew he probably shouldn't have come here without an invitation, but he might never get one. So he'd come to see Jeff on his own.

Along with age came some privileges.

He'd stopped by the Guthrie Ranch and talked with Lacey. She'd been in the corral working with the horses. He'd stood back and watched and had been impressed with her talent. He'd always thought it had been Trevor who had had the skill with the horses, but Lacey knew her way around those animals, too. Maybe Jeff's idea wasn't so bad. Those two could help each other.

He grinned. Who knows? Lacey Guthrie might even finally take notice of his grandson. At least, maybe she could help Jeff get through the rough time.

Avoiding several mesquite bushes, Hank continued toward the cabin on the hill. He parked and climbed out, then grabbed two shopping bags filled with things Maura and Ella had sent with him.

He made his way to the porch when Jeff came out. "Granddad. What are you doing here?"

"It was either me comin' here, or your mother and grandmother. And they'd probably be hanging ruffled curtains in the windows. So you got the best of the deal, me."

Jeff chuckled and took the bags.

"That's food, and in there are some towels. There's a cooler in the back of the truck."

"I'll get it later," Jeff said. "Come inside."

Hank walked through the door first. The place wasn't much bigger than a horse stall, but it was a lot cleaner.

The bunk against the wall was made up with white sheets and a green army blanket tucked in neatly on all sides. Two pairs of cowboy boots stood at the end. The one thing that looked out of place was a single crutch next to the door, reminding him of the months of pain and anguish his grandson had gone through during his time in the hospital.

Sadness hit Hank as he ambled over to the only place to sit down. He pulled out a chair. "So, looks like you've made the place real homey."

"It's not so bad."

"Sure, I believe you, but you know your mother isn't going to feel the same. An outside latrine and no shower isn't what they'd call civilized. So if you feel the need to get under a warm spray, come by the house."

Jeff couldn't help but smile. He always enjoyed Hank. Getting a grandfather was one of the best things about being adopted into the family.

"I'm going to rig up a portable shower out back."

"Good thing the weather is warm." The old man grew serious. "You know I have to report back to the ladies on how you're getting on. And I've learnt never to cross the women in this family, not if I ever want to eat again."

Jeff smiled. "Then you tell them that if I survived the deserts and the jungle, the Texas prairie isn't going to hurt me."

Grinning, Hank nodded. "I told 'em you'd be just fine."

"What else brings you up here, Granddad?"

Hank pushed his hat back off his forehead. "Well, I had this idea I wanted to run by you."

"I hope it doesn't have anything to do with moving home."

"No, I think if this is where you want to be, then it's the right place for you. My idea has something to do with Randell Corporation."

"And this concerns me how?"

"Just hear me out," Hank coaxed. "You know how we have guests that come to the ranch on vacation and want to work. They like the cowboy way of things."

"And it's always made money, too."

"I was thinking this year, at summer's end, I'd like to do an old-fashioned cattle drive. All guests on horseback, and we even have a chuck wagon with a cook to make the meals just like they did a hundred years ago. We can start at Chance's place and drive the cattle across to your dad's ranch. Then go on to Uncle Jarred and Aunt Dana's and onto Cade's lands, then finally end up at the Circle B. I have the quarters to house the guests."

"Sounds like you'd be going around in a circle."

"Almost. But we'd stay on private property, and if something does happen, we're not far from help." Hank raised an eyebrow. "So, what do you think?"

"Sounds good to me." Jeff was surprised his dad hadn't said anything. "How do the brothers like it?"

"I'll tell them eventually, but right now I want the grandkids on board first. And I want you to be in charge."

Jeff was caught off guard by this. "I can't do it."

"Why? You've been in the military for years, in charge of men, giving orders."

"I haven't been on a horse in a long time. Secondly, I don't even know if I can still ride."

"Sure you can. It's something you don't forget, especially since you were so good it. You could out-ride any of your cousins." Hank smiled. "Even then you strove to be the best."

Jeff knew he had drive. He'd proven it many times in the army, and it had saved his life more times than he could count. "That was before." He rubbed his thigh.

"Before what? The accident?" Hank shook his head. "You're just as good as before."

"The army doesn't think so," Jeff said bitterly. "They seem to think you need both legs to be a soldier."

CHAPTER THREE

EARLY in the morning, Jeff closed Fancy's gate. It had been a long time since he'd mucked out a stall. He didn't like it any better than he had as a kid.

He'd only been a horse owner for a few days, but he needed the physical work. Outside of his daily workouts, he'd been pretty sedentary lately, unlike the days when he used to take five-mile runs every morning. He couldn't handle that—yet.

He sat down on the bench next to the stall gate and rubbed his knee. Maybe he'd been pushing it. But that was how he did everything—to the hilt. He'd never held back, and he wasn't going to now.

"What's wrong with your leg?"

Jeff looked up find Colin standing nearby. Was the kid just lurking around, waiting to give him a bad time? "I'm just tired."

Those blue eyes narrowed. "You get shot in the army?"

Jeff gripped the railing and pulled himself up to stand. "Yeah, you could say that."

"Does it hurt?"

He didn't want to talk about this. "Sometimes. What are you doing out here?"

"Mom said I should help you. What do you want me to do?"

"What do you usually do?"

"Dad used to let me exercise the horses, but Mom only wants me to clean stalls."

"How about we do the cleaning first, then we'll see about the riding part."

If the boy was surprised at the answer, he didn't show it. "Whatever."

"Okay, let's start with the first two stalls. I need fresh straw spread out on the floors."

"Why? There aren't any horses."

"You've got a lot of questions, son. In the army, you don't ask, you just do."

"I'm too young to be in the army."

Jeff smiled. "Guess you're right. But there are two mares arriving tomorrow."

Thanks to his Uncle Chance spreading the word about the Guthrie Ranch being open for boarding and training, they already had their first two horses. The only problem was he wasn't sure he could handle it without help. "If you do a good job, we'll talk about wages."

The boy blinked. "You gonna *pay* me?"

Jeff nodded. "This is hard work. I'd like you to help out a few hours in the mornings. I need to learn my way around here. It's been a while since I handled horses. So, are you available?"

The kid couldn't hide his surprise. "Yeah. Do I get to help work the horses, too?"

"We need to talk to your mom about that. But from what I saw the other day, you're an experienced rider."

Colin puffed out his chest. "Since I was four years old. I'll be nine next month."

He liked the boy sharing that with him. "We still have to talk to your mom."

"Talk to me about what?"

They both turned around to find Lacey dressed in her uniform for her job at the supermarket. She came down the aisle. Her hair was pulled back into a serviceable ponytail, showing off her high cheekbones and bright-green eyes. Damn, if she didn't get his blood going.

He finally found his voice. "I've asked Colin if he wants to help me for a few hours a day. I was going to pay him."

"Can I, Mom?" The boy was excited. "Can I work with the horses?"

Lacey didn't look pleased with the idea. "We'll talk about it later. Why don't you go up to the house and wash up, Colin? Mindy's here to watch you and Emily while I go to work."

"Ah, Mom," he argued. "Why can't I help with the horses like I did with Dad?"

"Colin," Jeff began. "Your mom and I need to discuss this," he suggested, realizing his mistake of not telling Lacey about his idea first.

The boy's enthusiasm quickly died, and he turned and marched off.

Once alone, Lacey turned back to him, anger furrowing her eyebrows. "If you're trying to win my son over, you'll probably do it, especially when you dangle horses in his face."

"I wouldn't have, if I'd known how disrespectful he is to you. Why do you let him talk to you that way?"

Lacey didn't need this today. She'd purposely avoided Jeff since he'd been coming in the mornings.

She hadn't liked the feelings he'd created in her whenever he was around. Feelings she'd had to kill off years ago. "Colin has had a rough time since his dad's death."

"Most kids do, but you still need to rein the boy in."

"What makes you the expert?"

"I acted like a jerk at his age, too. Someone needs to take him in hand, and that means stop coddling him."

Her eyes widened. "He's only eight years old."

"Almost nine," he corrected her.

"He's not an army recruit, Jeff. He's still a little boy who's just lost his daddy."

"He also needs to learn respect for you. I don't think Trevor would have let him talk to you that way."

At the mention of her husband's name, sadness hit her. From the day Colin had been born, father and son had been inseparable. "Trevor would have handled it differently."

Jeff stiffened. "Sorry, I'm not Trevor."

Lacey tried to keep calm, but having Jeff around was making everything difficult. "Look, Gentry. We might be thrown together temporarily, but my family is *my* concern. Not yours. I'd appreciate it if you'd let me decide what's good for my son."

Jeff's dark gaze watched her for what seemed like an eternity. "Agreed," he finally said. "But there's something else we need to discuss."

She studied the man she'd practically grown up with. They'd shared childish secrets, survived adolescence, and he'd been her husband's best friend.

Her first lover.

Lacey glanced away. No, she couldn't think about that anymore. She couldn't let him know that it had been on her mind, either. Easy to say, harder to do when she'd been noticing the man far too much. The first thing she had to do was stop being so uptight whenever he was around.

"What…what do you want to talk about?" she asked.

"I think I've solved your problem with the ranch. Have you thought about taking on a partner?"

The next day Jeff stood back and gave the new portable shower a nod of approval. Not bad. The five-gallon container hung from a tree branch, directly over the canvas cubicle. At least now he could wash his entire body at one time. The hot summer sun would warm up the spring water quickly.

"So this is what you army guys call roughing it."

Jeff swung around, nearly losing his balance on the uneven ground, to find his cousin. A grinning Brandon Randell was dressed in the standard cowboy uniform of boots, jeans and a long-sleeved shirt to protect him from the Texas sun. He held the reins of his black quarter horse, Shadow.

"Well, I'll be damned." They exchanged a hearty hug. "What brings you out of the city, Detective Randell?" He glanced over his shoulder at the black stallion. "Just happened to be out for a ride?"

"I stopped by Hank's, and he told me you were staying up here." Brandon shrugged. "So Shadow and I cut through a couple of neighboring pastures and here we are. By car it would have been about a twenty-mile drive."

"So you did some trespassing," Jeff teased.

"I just tell people I'm on sheriff's business."

Brandon jammed his hands on his hips. "Besides, I need to come see how my cousin's doing."

Jeff had no doubt that Brandon had been sent to check on him. "Not bad," he told him. "I've lived in worse conditions. Best of all, I'm enjoying the peace and quiet."

Brandon smiled. "Surely you're not saying the Randell clan is too much for you?"

"I can handle them in small doses. Dad's been running interference for me."

"Take it from me, cuz, it's not going to stop a Randell. You know, eventually they're going to come looking for you." Brandon's smile disappeared. "Just know it's only because we all care about you. Man, it's good to have you home."

"It's good to be back." Jeff relaxed a little. He'd always gotten along with the oldest cousin. When Jeff, his mother and sister had first come here years ago, it had been Brandon's mother, Abby, who'd helped them find a place to live. They also shared the fact that their mothers had come from abusive backgrounds, and Randell men had come to their rescue.

Brandon led his horse to the creek for some water, and examined the shower structure. "Not bad. I guess you couldn't stand your own stink, huh?"

They both laughed. It felt good to Jeff. "You could say that."

Brandon was like all the Randell men—tall and broad-shouldered, with dark hair and eyes. There was also the distinguishing cleft chin that marked nearly all the male Randells. Brandon had surprised everyone after college by going into law enforcement instead of ranching. He was a detective with the sheriff's office.

"Granddad Hank said you bought two of the Guthrie's quarter horses at the auction and you're boarding them there."

"It seemed simpler to keep them there." Jeff started back up the rise toward the cabin. The hot afternoon sun beat down on his T-shirt-covered back, and his leg was tired from his long day. "The past year was rough on Lacey, or she would never have sold off her best quarter horses."

Brandon tipped his hat back. "I was sorry to hear about Trevor. Man, he was so young." Brandon shook his head. "And leaving a wife and young kids."

They reached the small porch partly shaded by a tree. "I heard you're a married man now. Congratulations."

"Thanks. When you're up to it, maybe you can meet Nora and Zach."

Jeff nodded. He wasn't making any promises.

"It's good you're around to help her," Brandon told him. "Lacey can use a friend."

Friend. He hadn't been much of one when Trevor had needed him. So far, he hadn't been doing well on that front with Lacey either. "I don't know how much good I can do." Jeff hated to admit to any kind of weakness. "Sometimes I think I have enough to deal with just taking care of myself."

Brandon paused. "Seems to me you've got a pretty good start. It takes time to adjust to your new life. You've started already, living up here alone."

Jeff frowned. "Alone? I think I've had more visitors here than I did at the house."

"Comes with the territory in this family. You wouldn't remember that because you've been gone so long."

"I guess I like my privacy."

"Isolating yourself isn't a good idea," Brandon pointed out.

Jeff wanted to argue, but instead he walked inside the cabin. The place was stifling. He grabbed two sodas from the cooler under the sink and went back outside to where Brandon sat under the shade.

"Thanks," his cousin said as he took the can and popped the top.

Careful of his leg, Jeff eased down beside him. Looking out at the horse grazing by the creek, he enjoyed the hint of a breeze from under the tree.

Brandon turned to him. "Look, Jeff. You have a right to live wherever you want. I'm the last one to preach, since I avoided the family ranch for years." His cousin gave him a sideways glance. "And I didn't have anything as life-changing as losing a leg happen."

Jeff flinched. Since being home, he hadn't talked about his loss, not even with his parents. Yet it seemed easier with Brandon. "I lost more than a leg. I lost my career. My identity. Special Forces was who I was." He looked down at his soda can. "Man, you'd think this was a beer, as much cryin' as I'm doing."

"I'm glad you're talking about it," his cousin said. "But you're wrong, Jeff. You might have lost your leg, and a career, but no, not your identity. There's a lot more to you, cuz, than being a soldier. And you have a family who loves you and we'll support you any way we can."

Jeff took a long drink of the sugary soda, trying to get rid of the lump in his throat. He couldn't lose it now. "Well, when you discover where I fit in, let me know."

"I think you've already found it. You own two fine

quarter horses and you're working with one of the prettiest and best trainers in these parts."

Jeff stiffened. He couldn't think of Lacey in that way, not anymore. "She's also my best friend's widow."

"So that's what's bothering you?"

"No," Jeff denied quickly. "What's bothering me is that I wasn't here when Trevor needed me. Now Lacey needs me."

"So that's why you bought two of her horses. To help her out?" Brandon stared out toward the pasture. "So are you going to be partners?" He turned to Jeff. "Are you going into the horse-breeding business?"

Jeff shrugged. "I'm not sure I can do more than clean stalls and feed the stock."

"Why not?" Brandon asked. "Years ago you were an exceptionally good horseman." Brandon smiled. "As I remember, you even broke a few mounts that summer we worked together."

That seemed like another lifetime ago. "I haven't been on a horse since I got back."

Brandon nodded and glanced down at the leg. "Seems to me if you can drive a vehicle, riding a horse shouldn't be difficult for a Special Forces guy. How much of your leg had to be amputated?"

His cousin had finally cut out the finesse, causing Jeff to tense before he forced himself to relax. "A few inches below the knee."

Brandon nodded. "I bet being in the military, you got the most hi-tech prosthesis."

He had. What the heck—he'd show Brandon. Jeff tugged his pant leg up, revealing his Justin short roper boot and the titanium limb that was connected to a plastic boot that covered his knee. "It's hard getting used to it. The hardest part is even after months, I still feel the loss, but it's been less and less. They call it phantom pain."

"I can't say I know how you feel, because I don't. But look at it this way; you nearly lost your life on that last mission. Just think how your mom and dad would be suffering if you hadn't made it back alive. All of us would be." Brandon's throat worked hard. "I never fought in a war, but I've known life-and-death situations. Far too many close calls over the years. Whatever you decide to do, I hope it's around here. I'd like to get to know you again." He broke out into a big grin. "I've never known a genuine hero."

Lacey was about at the end of her patience. When she got hold of Colin he was going to be grounded until the end of summer. If he lived that long.

She pulled the truck off the road and up toward the cabin. The last thing she wanted to do was disturb Jeff, but there wasn't any choice. Her son was missing and she had to find him.

She parked next to the familiar truck and headed up the rise, hoping Colin was here. Had Jeff been right? Did her son need a firmer hand? This was all new to her. She'd never had to worry about Colin's behavior before. She knew he'd been angry since his father's death, but it had only gotten worse. As much as she hated to, she needed to ask for help.

Lacey came around the side of the shack and found two men sitting on the edge of the porch. She recognized Brandon Randell right away. She hesitated to disturb them, but maybe the sheriff's detective could help, too. They were engrossed in conversation as she approached the porch. She saw they were both concentrating on Jeff's leg. She got closer and could see that it wasn't his leg, but a metal prosthesis. She gasped.

Both men turned toward her, and Jeff quickly pulled down his pant leg.

Brandon stood. "Lacey." He walked toward her and took her hand. "It's good to see you again."

"Hi, Brandon." She tried to gather her thoughts, but it was difficult. She glanced at Jeff, then started backing up. "I didn't mean to disturb you. I should go."

Jeff got to his feet and started after her. "Lacey, wait."

She did as he asked, but couldn't look at him. Oh, God, his leg. All this time she'd been harping on at him about not being around. What must he have gone through? She blinked at sudden tears.

Jeff's gaze narrowed. "Did you need me for something, Lacey?"

She opened her mouth, but her words were lost. What could she say?

"Lacey? What's wrong?"

Suddenly she remembered her reason for coming here. "I can't find Colin. I think he's run away."

CHAPTER FOUR

WHEN Jeff drew Lacey into his arms, he couldn't think about anything but calming her. Not how her soft and delicate body felt against his, or how many years he'd ached to hold her close like this. It was heaven and hell.

Right now he needed to concentrate on the problem at hand. He released her. "It's going to be okay, Lacey. We'll find Colin."

"When was the last time you saw your son?" Brandon asked, breaking into the moment.

Lacey's eyes widened. "It sounds terrible, but I'm not sure. When he came in from doing morning chores, we argued." She glanced at Jeff. "He talked again about working with the horses. I got upset with his attitude so I sent him upstairs." She brushed her hair back from her face. "About noon, I fixed him a sandwich and took it up to him, hoping we could work it out." She blinked back fresh tears. "He was gone."

"What about Emily?" Jeff asked. "Did she see him leave?"

Lacey shook her head. "She's been at her friend's house all day."

Jeff watched as she tried to stay in control. "Did you

check the barn?" he asked. "Maybe he was just hiding out."

She folded her arms. "I checked and found his horse gone, too. I don't know how I missed him. I was in the kitchen most of the morning. He must have walked Buddy around the front of the house so I wouldn't see him leave." Her lower lip quivered. "He wanted to get away from me that badly."

"He's had a rough year, Lacey," Brandon said. "But we're going to find him." He frowned. "Are you sure you've checked all the places he would go?"

She nodded. "That's why I came up here. This was where he used to come with Trevor."

Jeff's gut tightened. "Had he been upset that I moved in?"

She began wringing her hands. "I don't know any more. Colin seems to be mad at everything and everyone lately. He hated that I had to sell Rebel and Fancy."

Jeff pulled out his cell phone. "I'll call Dad and get some of the family out looking for him."

Brandon also reached for his radio and made a call to Granddad Hank. Jeff knew that the Randells wouldn't hesitate to help in the search, especially for a lost child.

Brandon hung up. "I think we'll come up with enough manpower to search for a few hours. If we don't find him by then, we'll handle it as a runaway. I'll need a picture of Colin and I'll alert the sheriff of the situation." He held up a hand. "It's just a precaution for now."

Lacey wiped her eyes and nodded. "I have a school photo in my purse." She walked off to the truck.

Brandon faced Jeff. "I can make better time if I borrow your pickup."

"Sure, the keys are on the console," Jeff agreed. "What about your horse?"

"Could you put Shadow in the lean-to? I'll send a ranch hand up to get him."

Lacey returned and handed Brandon the wallet-sized picture of Colin.

"Good-looking boy." Brandon smiled as he examined the photo. "I know it's useless to tell you to go home and wait, so I won't."

"We'll go look together." Jeff nodded to Lacey. He hated feeling helpless. Hell, his job in the military had been tracking people.

Brandon walked to the truck and took off. Once alone, Jeff glanced at Lacey and caught her looking at him. It just wasn't the way he'd always hoped she would.

He might as well get it out in the open. "I haven't been on a horse since I lost my leg." There, he'd said it. "But we can search a lot of territory by truck. We both know the area pretty well."

Stunned, Lacey watched as Jeff started off toward the creek. Focusing her attention on his stride, she finally noticed the slight limp. She closed her eyes, thinking about all he must have gone through. Especially the pain.

Oh, God. The terrible things she'd said to him. All the time he'd been in a hospital, going through his own hell. No one had said a word to her and Trevor about it.

Well, there were going to be words now. She caught up with him as he took hold of Shadow's reins.

"Why didn't you tell me?"

He didn't look at her as he led the large animal up

the slight rise toward the cabin. "What was there to say, Lacey? Oh, by the way, I lost a leg during my last mission." He shot her a glare. "There are thousands of men and women who've come home in worse shape them me. I only lost the lower part of my leg. Some lost both, some lost arms…so I'm one of the fortunate ones."

"You are," she told him. "You made it home." She hesitated. "But, Jeff, I said some awful things to you."

"So because now you know I'm an amputee you're going to be nicer to me?"

She cringed. "No. I just couldn't understand why you weren't here. I thought you stayed away because you just couldn't face coming back to see Trevor."

"Forget it, Lacey. I deserved it. I didn't come and see Trevor as much as I should have. But don't ever doubt that I loved him like a brother. I'll always regret that I couldn't be here for him, or you."

Lacey stiffened. Had Jeff ever regretted not being there for her ten years ago?

They made it to the rough wood lean-to, and Jeff tied the horse to the post, then flipped the stirrup over the saddle and began to loosen the cinch. Once finished, he pulled the saddle off the horse and put it on the railing.

"Deep down I knew that," she said, wondering how much her husband had wanted to see his friend. "I guess I wanted you there to ease Trevor's fears." She felt her emotions stirring again. "You were the level-headed one, never afraid of anything."

Jeff's dark gaze met hers. "Hell, Lacey, we're all afraid sometime. And I'm afraid right now that my moving up here might have pushed Colin away more."

Lacey shook her head. She was the one feeling threatened that Jeff was back, and living so close. "No, my son has been angry for a long time. He misses his dad. At one time we were a close family."

Jeff studied her. "Of course. You and Trevor have loved each other since high school."

She avoided his gaze. There had been many rough patches in their marriage, but what was the point of dredging that up now?

He patted the horse. "You were the perfect couple."

"We all know how looks can be deceiving," she said quietly.

For the past two hours, Jeff had driven around the area, going everywhere possible. If Colin was on horseback, he doubted they'd find him along the road. He called Brandon, who informed them that several of the Randells were out looking for the boy. The only problem was that nightfall was closing in on the search efforts.

Jeff pulled Lacey's Jeep up beside the cabin. They got down as Lacey took out her cell phone and called back to her house.

He walked to the cabin, praying that the boy had come to his senses and was waiting for them inside. When he saw the empty room he knew from experience that there was a possibility Colin could be in trouble. He sincerely hoped the child was just plain stubborn.

Lacey appeared behind him. "Brandon told me that there's quite a group of people at my house." She sighed, leaning against the table. "I can't face them, Jeff."

He felt completely helpless. He wasn't used to standing around and doing nothing. "Are you sure there isn't anywhere else the boy could be? Did he and Trevor go riding anywhere special?"

She shook her head.

"Did he ever mention a name? A landmark?"

She shook her head, but then her eyes began to widen. "Wait! There was a place that Trevor took Colin camping."

"Where?"

"I'm not sure, only that it's on the property." She paused. "And they called it their secret place. I didn't want to intrude, so I never pushed for a location."

Jeff tried to remember all the places he'd gone with Trevor when they were kids. They'd both loved to investigate everything, and they'd pretty much had free rein of the ranch. Suddenly he recalled a place along the back of the Guthrie property. A rock formation. It was so cool; they'd sworn never to tell anyone. He guessed Trevor had never even told Lacey.

"Did Trevor ever mention a place called Three Rock Ridge?"

She looked thoughtful. "I did overhear him mention that name once. Oh, Jeff, do you think Colin went there?"

His spirits brightened, too. "I'm not sure, but I'm going to find out." He walked through the door, around to the lean-to and Brandon's horse. After tossing the blanket over Shadow's back, he reached for the saddle before Lacey showed up.

"What are you doing?" she asked.

"I'm going to find Colin," he told her.

"You can't, Jeff. I'll call Brandon."

He turned to her. "Why? Don't you think I'm capable of finding your son?"

"It's not that," she said, then paused. "It's just you've only gotten out of the hospital—"

"And I don't have a leg anymore so I can't possibly do anything," he finished for her flatly.

"No, that's not what I meant." She gripped his hand. "You said it yourself, you haven't been on a horse in a long time. What if something happens to you out there?"

"Nothing is going to happen to me, I know where I'm going."

"Then wait for Brandon," she pleaded.

"I'm asking you to trust me on this. We don't have time to lose, Lace. We're running out of daylight, fast."

Jeff continued to tighten the cinch, adjusting the stirrups before leading the horse out. He slipped his right foot into the stirrup, grabbed the pommel and pulled himself up into the saddle. His heart raced as he glanced down at his left leg and guided it into the other stirrup. There was no doubt that it felt strange, but he quickly took control of the spirited animal. He tugged on the reins, putting the horse through long-remembered commands.

He looked down at her. "Tell Brandon I'm heading northeast about two miles from here. I have my cell phone and I'll call you when I get there."

Lacey came up to the horse and placed her hand on his leg, just above his knee. "Jeff..."

Her touch bothered him more than he wanted it to. He'd hoped over the years that his feelings for her had faded. They obviously hadn't. "I'll bring your son back, Lacey. I promise."

"You don't have to do this," she insisted.

She had no idea. "Yes, I do. I owe this to Trevor."

* * *

Thirty minutes later, Jeff's muscles were tensed, and fatigue had set in. Man, he seemed to have forgotten his years of training. He'd run off without even a flashlight on him. Great, he could see the headlines now: Special Forces Soldier Gets Lost While Looking for Missing Boy.

As the sun began to set behind the trees, he finally came up to the familiar rock formation. So far, there was no sign of the boy—then he smelled the smoke. A campfire. He swung his leg over the back of the horse, and carefully climbed down. Once he got his footing, he led the animal to the other side of the boulders.

He stopped, and his heart lurched at the sight of the boy sitting by a small campfire in the clearing. His saddle and blanket were arranged in a makeshift bed. Nearby, his horse, Buddy, was hobbled and grazing in a patch of grass. So the kid knew how to take care of himself.

Jeff stepped out into the open. "Looks like all the comforts of home."

Colin jumped up, looking guilty, then turned on the attitude. "What are you doing here?"

"I'll give you three guesses." With a tug on Shadow's reins, he walked into camp. "You have to know how worried your mom is."

The boy shrugged and sat down. "She treats me like a baby."

"Maybe that's because you keep acting like one," Jeff pointed out. "Pulling this stunt wasn't a wise choice."

Colin threw him a killer look. "She won't let me do *anything*."

"Like I said, you have to prove yourself first. And your actions lately haven't been exactly mature."

"What do you know? You're not my dad." He turned away, his eyes filled with tears.

"I know, Colin, but can't I be your friend? To start with, I know why you're acting like this."

"You don't know nothin'."

"I do, because I acted the same way when my mother brought me here to live, and my dad wasn't in my life," Jeff explained.

"Did he die?" Colin asked curiously.

Jeff shook his head. "No, he went to prison." He hadn't thought about his biological father, Darren Wells, in years. "But that didn't mean I didn't want him around. Boys need their dads."

He saw the boy blink at tears. "Well, I don't need one anymore."

Jeff's chest tightened, knowing what Colin was going through. "Yeah, I can see that." He glanced around. "By the looks of it, you're doing fine on your own. Are you planning on living off the land?"

"No. I just need to think about things."

"Anything I can help you with?"

The boy shook his head.

Jeff released a breath and motioned to the log. "Would you mind if I sit for a while? My leg isn't used to riding yet." He rubbed his thigh, happy he'd accomplished the task, then took a seat on the log.

"What's wrong with your leg?" Those eyes, so like Trevor's, studied him. "Did you get wounded or something?"

"Yes, I did, but the doctors couldn't save it."

The boy swallowed. "You mean you don't have a leg?"

There was no more hiding for him. "They removed it just below my knee."

"Wow," the boy sighed in wonder. "Can I see?"

Jeff couldn't help but be taken aback. Colin was definitely Trevor's son. He reached down and tugged up his pant leg, once again exposing the metal post.

Colin leaned closer to examine it. "Does it hurt?"

"Sometimes. It's been nine months, but I'm still learning to walk with the prosthesis."

"Cool. Do you ever take it off?"

Jeff nodded. "When I shower and sleep."

"Will you take it off now?"

Okay, this was more than he'd expected. He hadn't shown anyone this besides medical personnel. He examined the boy's wide-eyed look. Jeff realized Colin wouldn't judge him, or even make fun of him. He was just curious.

"I'll make a deal with you. I'll call your mother and you tell her you're safe, and then I'll show you."

Colin groaned. "She's going to be mad. And she'll ground me until school starts."

"What you did was wrong and dangerous. So you've got to deal with that."

The boy nodded. "Okay, but you've got to stay with me here until morning."

Jeff gave him his best stern look, thinking about the hard ground.

"It's already too dark to go back now," Colin pointed out.

The boy was too smart for his own good. "I'll say one thing, kid, you remind me far too much of your dad. He used to get me into trouble, too."

Colin flashed a bright grin. Jeff was suddenly taken back twenty years. He had a feeling Trevor would have loved this idea.

Early the next morning, Lacey waited at the cabin for her son's return. She had been against letting Colin stay out there, but Jeff had assured her they were both safe. Yet one night out didn't solve their problems, not with her son, and not for the future.

Lacey drew a breath and paced the small cabin. How was she going to handle this? Colin couldn't get off without a punishment. She sighed. "Oh, Trevor, what do I do? I'm not sure if I can handle raising a boy on my own."

At the sink, she glanced out of the window toward the pasture. Still no one. She looked down at her hand resting on the counter and the letters carved in the wood.

She smiled and began tracing the chiseled-out letters, remembering all those years ago. She'd been new in San Angelo when Trevor Guthrie had come up to her in seventh grade and introduced himself. There had never been anything shy about him. From that moment they'd become friends. In high school things changed and they became a couple. From the first, Trevor had been her friend, protector and so much more.

She traced the other name. Jeff. "Jeff Gentry," she breathed.

He was as opposite from Trevor as you could get. She would label him the strong, silent type, along with dark and dangerously handsome. The two boys had been best friends from an early age. Then she'd moved in. There were times when she wondered if Jeff had resented her for that.

Sometimes she'd caught him looking at her.

Nothing that had ever spooked her, but his gaze just caused strange feelings inside her. Then, after graduation, Jeff's plans had been to go away to college. The only thing Trevor ever wanted had been to take over his father's horse-breeding business. She'd also spent a lot of her time at the ranch, helping him with the training while taking college courses locally.

She and Trevor had gotten even closer that year. He talked about marriage. After having lived through her own parents' divorce, Lacey had wanted to wait a while. They'd argued about it a lot, eventually breaking up.

During that time, Jeff came home from college for the summer. He'd contacted her and asked her to meet him at the cabin. Lacey went, surprised at the change in him. He'd filled out, literally turning into a man.

When he started pitching to her about what a great guy Trevor was, she'd gotten angry, telling him that she needed some time and space. She'd told him she wanted to date other guys since she'd never had a chance to before. Feeling furious that Trevor had sent Jeff to plead his case, she'd slipped her arms around him and kissed him. To this day she couldn't believe she'd done something so crazy. What she did remember was that it had been an unbelievable kiss. By the time Jeff had released her, she could barely stand without swaying.

"Lace, this is wrong," he had told her, but he still had kissed her again. Soon they couldn't get enough of one another and had ended up making love on the single bunk. Lacey had suddenly realized her strong feelings for Jeff.

But afterward Jeff could barely look at her. He'd told her he was sorry about what happened. When she'd tried to tell him that *she* wasn't sorry, he'd informed her he was going into the military. Then he'd left the cabin, and she'd stayed and cried her eyes out.

Over the next few weeks, Jeff had been scarcely around and she'd been miserable. She was in love with a man who wanted nothing to do with her.

Jeff had finally left town without even seeing her. Trevor came to see her, though. In her pain, she'd realized that he was the one who truly loved her—and so three months later she'd married him.

Over the years Jeff had only made it home about half a dozen times. She'd made excuses not to see him. Trevor had kept in touch by e-mail or gone to visit Jeff on base a few times, but that had only lasted those first couple of years. Then there'd been nothing from him at all.

Her marriage with Trevor had gone through some rough times. Lacey hated the fact that what had happened that summer could have caused her husband pain. Trevor was a good man. The man who'd stood by her. Lacey had tried to be a good wife to make up for what was lacking in their marriage.

But there would always be that summer. That night she and Jeff had betrayed Trevor.

"Mom?"

Lacey swung around to see Colin standing at the door. Her heart began to pound hard. He was safe. She rushed to him. "Oh, Colin." She didn't want to think about the possibility she could have lost him. She held him tightly as Jeff walked through the door.

"Thank you," she managed. "Thank you for bringing my son back."

Jeff nodded. "Colin, I believe you have something to say to your mother."

The boy lowered his head and began to murmur.

Jeff came in. "Speak up, son, so she can hear you."

Colin raised his head, his blue eyes sad. "I'm sorry I ran away, Mom, and that I worried you. I won't do it again."

Lacey glanced at Jeff then back at her son. "Yes, you did worry me, Colin. How can I trust you when you run away because things don't go your way? And there were so many people out looking for you."

"I know. It was a stupid thing to do. Jeff said I need to act my age and help you more 'cause you have a lot on your shoulders."

She tried not to act surprised at her son's newfound understanding. "Well, not any more than I can handle."

"I'm going to do more," he promised. "If you say it's okay, I'll help Jeff with the horses and clean out the stalls."

"Sounds like a good idea. And it looks like that's all you'll be doing since you'll be serving a two-week punishment. That means you can't ride Buddy, or any other horse." She started to leave but stopped. "And no video games or television, either." Lacey walked out, hearing her son's groans.

"I warned you," Jeff told him. "Never make your mother worry."

"I bet Mom's tougher than being in the army."

She heard a laugh from Jeff, before he said, "No way, your mom's much better. No sergeant I ever knew gave me hugs and kisses."

CHAPTER FIVE

EARLY one morning the following week, Jeff arrived at the Guthrie Ranch. When he got out of the truck, he spotted a horse and rider in the corral.

The air in his lungs seemed to stop as he watched the vision on horseback. It was Lacey riding Fancy. She sat atop the beautiful liver-chestnut filly, her shoulders and hands relaxed as her long jeans-clad legs easily controlled the horse's movements.

Jeff stood on the bottom rung of the railing, unable to take his eyes off her. Her blouse hung open, revealing a tank top underneath. A honey-blond ponytail was pulled through the back of a Texas Longhorns baseball cap and swinging freely while she rode around the arena, putting the animal through its paces.

He'd had no idea she could ride like this. When Lacey had moved here, she and her divorced mother had lived in town. As kids they all rode, Lacey usually doubled up with Trevor, so Jeff had never got to see her hidden talents. He studied her closely, enjoying her grace and ability. This wasn't something you could teach a person.

"Hey, Jeff."

Hearing Colin call out his name got Lacey's attention, too. The private show was over.

"Hey, kid." Jeff got off the railing and went through the corral gate. "Morning, Lacey," he called to her as he walked into the arena.

She climbed off Fancy and led the horse toward him. "Good morning," she returned, looking embarrassed, as if she'd been caught doing something wrong. "I didn't expect you so early."

"I thought I'd get started before the day heated up," he said, feeling the warmth already, though it had nothing to do with the sun. "Why didn't you tell me you could ride like that?"

She shrugged, but before she could speak, Colin showed up and took over the conversation. "Mom used to show horses. Dad said she has talent."

"Colin," Lacey began. "Aren't you supposed to be in the house watching your sister?"

"Ah, Mom. I want to help Jeff."

"And you will, but your punishment isn't over yet. You still have another week."

Colin looked at Jeff for support. "Sorry, buddy. I can't help you on this one. You did the crime and now you have to do the time."

The boy nodded. "Are you still going to pay me to work with you next week?"

Jeff stole a glance at Lacey. "I have to discuss it with your mother first."

The boy looked at his mother and began to say something, but stopped when she raised her hand.

"Not now, Colin," she said. "I told you my decision will be made when I see how you handle yourself in the next seven days."

The boy nodded. "Okay, I'll watch Emily and clean my room. Then I'll do the dishes." With a wave, he ran off toward the house.

Jeff watched Colin leave and smiled. "Darn, the boy works all the angles, doesn't he?"

"I guess you can say, 'like father, like son,'" she said, finding herself smiling, too. "Together they would gang up on me and I didn't stand a chance."

He looked at her. "How's he been this past week?"

"Not too bad. He has his moments."

"If you want I'll talk to him again," he offered.

She shook her head. "No, thanks, I can handle my children." She turned and tugged on Fancy's reins as she headed toward the barn.

Jeff caught up with her. "Hey, I didn't mean to cause a problem."

"Look, Jeff. Emily and Colin are *my* responsibility. I'm the one who's raising them, so I'm the one who disciplines them."

Lacey had tried to stay away from the barn whenever Jeff came around. She didn't want to confront her feelings since his return. It had been more than she wanted to admit. The one thing she could do was keep him out of her personal life.

She opened Fancy's stall and put her inside, then began removing the tack. What was wrong with her? Jeff had found her runaway son, and bought two of her horses. Now, he was paying to board them here.

But what she didn't want was another man handling everything for her. Not again.

She looked up from her task to find him leaning against the open stall gate. He looked too good at six in the morning, with his fitted green army T-shirt and worn jeans. That was the problem, she was noticing far too much about Jeff Gentry. Still, that wasn't a reason to be rude.

"Sorry, I shouldn't have said that. You went out and found Colin and you're helping me out here."

"I don't want your *gratitude,* Lace. What I need is a partner."

Jeff had always liked the Guthries' kitchen. The maple table was placed in the center of the bright-yellow room. The cabinets were a knotty pine with fifties-style brown Formica covering the counters. The white appliances weren't in much better shape. Nothing had changed since they were kids.

Had Trevor done poorly with the business? The outside of the house could use some paint, although the barn and corrals were in great shape.

Lacey filled two cups at the coffeemaker, then brought them to the table and sat down. He took a seat across from her.

She sighed. "I thought we already settled this. I can't afford to continue with the breeding business. I can't take that much time away from the kids."

"You could if you quit your job in town."

She shook her head. "I need the health insurance, especially for the kids. My hours are cut to the bare minimum to even qualify for it at the supermarket as it is. I can't afford to buy it on my own."

"You could if we got a group policy for the business. I believe we only need three employees." He shrugged. "We can hire someone to help out, for feeding and exercising the horses. With help we can bring in more boarders. That means more monthly income."

Jeff paused to watch her. Good. She was thinking about it.

"What do you want me to do?" she asked.

"I want you to do what you're good at, the training. I had no idea you were so accomplished."

"Trevor was the one with the talent." She shrugged. "He taught me. When I got good enough, I began working with the horses on my own."

"From what I've seen, lady, I'd say you were damn good."

"I've had some success. Trevor was the one who built the reputation. I'm afraid that people won't be as willing to trust me without him here."

"They will when they see you ride."

"We need horses for that to happen, and we only have three. Since Bonnie is Rebel's dam that eliminates her."

"Would you be opposed to talking with my Uncle Chance?"

She blinked in surprise. "Chance Randell?"

He nodded. "Maybe we can work a business deal with him. Granddad said he's impressed with Rebel and Fancy. There's also my Aunt Tess. Of course, she's more involved with the training end of it."

Lacey had admired Tess Meyers Randell for years. "She's one of the top trainers in Texas. How many reining champions has she bred and trained?"

"I'm not sure. But I know Brandon used to help her when she only had one horse. In the past few years, she's cut her business down considerably. I bet she'll be willing to give us some pointers."

Lacey studied Jeff. Suddenly he wanted to go into the quarter horse business. "Jeff, why are you really doing this? I mean, why not eliminate me as competition and team up with your uncle?"

He took a long drink from his mug. "To be honest, I want to stay out of the family business for now."

Did he have any idea how lucky he was? "They're your family, Jeff. They love you. They just want to help you."

His eyes narrowed. "I like to do things on my own."

Stubborn man. "You just said you wanted me as a partner."

"I want to prove to myself I can make it on my own. But I need your help and talent, too, Lace." He glanced away. "I'm not sure I can handle the hours on horseback."

She doubted that. "You'd be surprised, Jeff. You've always been able to do anything you put your mind to."

He sucked in a breath. "I'm not the same man you once knew."

Had she ever really known Jeff? "None of us are the same."

He studied her, but didn't say anything.

"But I know what courage it took to get up on that horse the night you went off to find Colin."

She saw the flash of pain in his eyes as he got to his feet. "I need to get to work." He started toward the door. "I'm going over to Chance's place. I just need you to tell me you'll give the partnership a try."

She was crazy, no, insane, even to think about risking any more with this man, especially her heart. She couldn't speak, because even with the risks, something made her want to take this chance, rationalizing that this would be for Colin and Emily. But deep down, she wanted it for herself, too.

She looked at Jeff and nodded. "I'll think about it."

* * *

Later that day, Jeff pulled up to the restored Victorian house at the Randell ranch. Chance was the eldest of the three Randell brothers, then came Cade and Travis. Years ago when their father, Jack, had been sent away for cattle rustling, Chance had tried to keep them all together, but the courts wouldn't allow a minor to take responsibility for his siblings. That's when widower Hank Barrett had stepped in and become their foster parent. They'd been family ever since, even adding Jack's three illegitimate sons, Jarred, Wyatt and Dylan, to the clan.

Chance came out of the back door followed by his petite wife, Joy. The couple had been happily married for years and it showed. Like Jeff's own parents, they were crazy about each other.

Chance hurried down the steps. "Hey, nephew, it's about time you came out of hiding." He gathered Jeff in a tight hug. "It's good to have you home."

"I'm taking it slow," Jeff managed, not having realized how emotional he'd feel at seeing his uncle again.

Chance stood back and looked him over. "Not too bad. I heard you got shot up pretty good."

Jeff didn't want to talk about it at the moment. "I survived."

There was a flash of sadness across Chance's face. "Sorry about the leg." Just as quickly he brightened. "You can't keep a Randell down for long, though."

Jeff laughed, covering up the still-vivid memories of his months in the hospital. "No, I guess you can't."

Joy, a pretty blonde, then came up and offered him a hug, too. "I'm glad you're home safe, Jeff. I know your mom is over the moon."

"If her cooking up a storm is any indication, yes, I'd say she's happy to have me back."

Joy made Jeff promise to stop by for supper one night, before returning to the house.

They watched her leave, then Chance turned to him. "I talked to your dad and he said you bought two Guthrie quarter horses."

"Yeah, Rebel Run and Doc's Fancy Girl."

Chance let out a long whistle. "Man, I tried to get my hands on that pair a while back." He frowned. "I take it Lacey Guthrie is having a rough time."

Jeff nodded. "Yeah, I'm hoping that's going to change. I've asked her to be a partner."

His uncle didn't look surprised. "So what are your plans?"

"That depends on you. Seems I'm going to need some stud service."

Chance laughed as he shoved his cowboy hat off his forehead. His sandy-brown hair was streaked with gray. "This sounds interesting."

Jeff explained the situation as they headed toward the large barn. Chance Randell's quarter horses were top grade around the area. He didn't train them for show, only as riding mounts and some cutting horses.

"We need to build up our barn stock," Jeff told him as they went into the cool barn. "I want Lacey to continue to do the training, but we need foals. How do you feel about making a deal? Give me stud service for Bonnie. In trade, Rebel will cover two of your mares."

"That sounds like a possibility." Chance rubbed the back of his neck. "Another is why not just sell Rebel's semen?"

Jeff began to realize that ten years in the military

wasn't going to help him in this new venture. "I hadn't thought that far ahead, but that's an idea."

"Jeff, I'll do whatever I can to help you out." Chance grinned. "And it wouldn't be a hardship at all to get a couple of foals sired by Rebel."

"So it's a deal?"

His uncle held out his hand. "Welcome to the horse-breeding business."

The next afternoon at the cabin, Jeff was tired, not to mention hot and dirty from his morning at the Guthrie Ranch. He needed a shower in the worst way.

After stripping off his clothes and prosthesis, he grabbed his crutch, a towel and shaving kit, then made his way down to the creek. The intense heat was peaking, but he kept his focus on the thought of the cool, clear water. Too bad it wasn't deep enough to swim in. With the crutch under his arm for support, he reached the large rock he'd moved a few days ago so he could sit down to wash.

With a sigh, he then scooped up creek water with an old pan he'd found in the cabin, and poured it over his head. The cold water made him gasp, then smile. Heaven. After a few more scoops, he grabbed a bar of soap and began to scrub the filth off his body. Once lathered up, he reached for his crutch, stood and made his way to the shower. Inside the canvas flap, he reached up and opened the valve and let the trickling water rinse him off.

He was starting to feel like a new man.

Lacey closed the Jeep's door and walked up the hill to the cabin. She'd been trying to reach Jeff by cell phone, but there wasn't any answer. It kept going straight to voice mail. And she needed to talk to him right away, before he started making any permanent plans for the business.

There wasn't going to be a partnership, because there wasn't going to be a ranch. Not since today's mail had brought a notice from the bank, stating a payment was due in two weeks. The sum was an unbelievable amount. She didn't recall any loan that was due. Nor did she have that kind of money to pay it off. There had to be a mistake.

During a call to the bank and a long discussion with a Mr. Dixon, she had learned Trevor had taken out the loan about eighteen months ago. What hurt the most was that her husband hadn't even discussed it with her. He'd even forged her name on the loan papers. He'd used the ranch as collateral to borrow for the business.

She didn't have a way to come up with the money to pay off the loan. She was going to lose her home.

What was she going to tell Jeff? Pride wouldn't allow her to say her own husband didn't trust her enough to share their troubles. She had to come up with another reason to pull out of their partnership.

She struggled with threatening tears. For the first time in nearly a year she'd started to hope again. She was going to get to do what she truly enjoyed, train horses and provide security for her kids. Now, once again, she had to fight to keep a roof over her family's head.

At the cabin, she found the door partly opened. "Jeff?" With no answer, she peered inside. The neatly organized room was empty and Jeff was nowhere in sight. She started to leave when she caught sight of a pair of jeans at the end of the bunk alongside his boots, one still with the metal prosthesis attached to it.

Sadness washed over her as she thought about the agony Jeff had to have gone through. She didn't know any details about his accident, but it must have been life-or-death for the doctors to remove his leg. She felt a tear on her cheek and brushed it away. So much had changed in just a year. While Trevor had been fighting to live, it seemed Jeff had been, too. Was he just trying to make up for the past, for not being here when his best friend was dying?

Lacey had carried the guilt as well. But this was different. She wasn't Jeff's responsibility. Maybe finding the loan papers was the disconnection she needed. She couldn't let Jeff get drawn any closer to her.

Lacey walked out of the cabin. She had to get out of here before Jeff came back, but she couldn't leave without making sure he was okay. Halfway to the creek she saw the top of his head in a portable shower. How did he do that, standing on one leg?

It wasn't her business. She quietly backed away, hoping he hadn't noticed her. Before she got back up the slope, she heard a curse and looked over her shoulder. The shower had collapsed to the ground, taking Jeff with it.

She rushed toward the creek and knelt down beside him. "Jeff! Jeff, are you okay?" She worked to open the canvas flap.

His head shot up with a groan. "Lace? What the hell are you doing here?"

"I was looking for you. You need me to help you."

"No, I don't need your help. Just go."

His short hair was spiky, his face unshaven. He looked good in a rough-guy sort of way. "I can handle it."

"I can't leave you like this." She looked around and saw an abandoned crutch by the stream. "At least let me help you up."

"No!" He sat up and the canvas fell, exposing his muscular chest and washboard abs. He pointed to the spot just out of his reach. "Just hand me the crutch and leave."

Don't think about this gorgeous man, she told herself. She finally tore her gaze away and went to get what he asked for. "Someone's got to help you to the cabin."

His dark eyes locked with hers. "Then you're going to be waiting a long time, lady."

"You are the most bull-headed man," she sighed.

"And you are one seriously stubborn woman. I can do this myself."

"And I'm going to make sure that you don't hurt yourself any further." She glanced down at his body. She gasped. He was naked. Of course he was—he'd been showering!

Her eyes met his narrow gaze. "That's right, Lace. You're going to get an eyeful if you hang around much longer."

She swallowed as she realized she was practically lying on top of the man. She could feel his heat, the hardness of his body. "I only want to help you," she managed.

"And I'm telling you, I don't need it." His gaze darkened even more as it lowered to her mouth. "Unless you want to take care of my other needs."

"Hey, you two."

They both turned as Brandon came toward them. "And here I was worried about you." He grinned. "I can see you're both in good hands."

CHAPTER SIX

DAMN. The last thing Jeff wanted was an audience.

"Not funny. Why don't you both leave? I've got this under control."

He glared at Brandon, hoping he'd understand and take Lacey with him, but neither one of them moved.

Lacey looked at Jeff. "Since Brandon's here to help you, I'll go." She turned and marched off.

Once he heard the truck start, he breathed a sigh and, naked as the day he was born, got up onto his knees. "Grab me that towel, would you?"

"Not a problem." Brandon did as he asked and handed it to him with a grin. "Anything to keep from looking at your skinny butt."

Jeff couldn't help but smile. "You were always jealous 'cause the girls liked mine better in jeans."

"What is this, high school?"

Sometimes he wished it was. Life was so much simpler. With the towel secured around his waist, Jeff reached for the crutch, then pulled himself up with ease. Once he got his balance, they headed to the cabin.

Jeff walked inside with Brandon following him. "So you want to tell me what was going on with Lacey?" his cousin asked.

"Nothing. She just showed up." Jeff sat down on the bunk and slipped on a pair of boxers, then his jeans. Securing the prosthesis boot over his stump, he stood and pulled them up. After buttoning the fly, he walked to the kitchen area and took two cold cans of soda from the cooler, and handed Brandon one. "Just like you did."

"We're cousins. Do I need an excuse to stop by?"

Jeff studied him awhile. "Are you going to tell me I should move home where someone can take care of me?"

Brandon cocked an eyebrow. "Why should I do that? You seemed to handle things." He took a drink of soda. "And besides, you've got Lacey showing up to check on you."

Jeff glanced away. "Ending up butt-naked on the ground isn't the way to impress a woman."

Brandon's smile grew bigger. "That depends on how you want to impress her."

Jeff stared. He wasn't going to go there. He'd stepped over the line once before, never again. "She's my friend's wife."

"Was," his cousin corrected. "Trevor's been gone nearly a year."

Jeff was surprised at Brandon's suggestion. He shook his head. "It wouldn't be right."

"Says who?"

"Me." He turned and looked out of the window above the sink. He loved this view. Would he ever get over the guilt? "I can't think about this now."

"Why, because you lost a leg?"

Jeff's fingers gripped the counter. "That's part of it. Another is I don't exactly have a career."

"None of that will matter to the right woman." He

paused. "Not to someone like Lacey. She cares about you, Jeff, and if you're honest you care about her, too."

"Of course I do, she and Trevor were my friends." He couldn't just blurt out his feelings for Lacey. "My main focus is trying to figure out how I'm going to fit in here." He turned to his cousin. "In case you haven't noticed, my life has changed drastically in the past year."

Brandon nodded. "And know that we're your family and we love you. We're just happy to have you back."

Brandon watched him for a few seconds. "That brings me to why I stopped by. I want you to meet my wife, Nora. We'd like you to come to dinner."

Jeff didn't want to do the single-guy-comes-to-dinner thing. "I don't know if I'm ready."

"You'll never be ready. Just jump in. Hey, it's not a big family dinner, only Nora, myself and Zach." Brandon looked thoughtful. "If you don't want to come alone, bring Lacey and her kids. Colin is about Zach's age."

Bring Lacey as his date? That could change things between them. Not that there was anything between them, or ever would be. He suddenly flashed back to the creek and how it felt having her body pressed against his. A thrill raced through him, but he shook it off.

"I don't know if I'm ready to get close to a woman."

Brandon gave him an incredulous look. "From what I saw out there between the two of you, I'd say you're pretty much there already."

Hours later, Lacey was still pacing the office at the house. Colin was up in his room and Emily was in the family room playing with her dolls.

That gave her too much time to wonder about the bank's next move. Would they evict her in two weeks?

Would she have time to find a place for the horses, as well as an apartment? She began to shake, knowing she couldn't do anything to stop her world from falling apart. She'd already used most of the auction money to cover Trevor's hospital bills.

Anger and fear took over. "Oh, Trevor, how could you leave me with this mess?"

"Lacey?"

She turned around to find Jeff standing in the doorway. What was he doing here? "Jeff."

"Your back door was open and I called out, Colin let me in," he explained. "What was so important you needed to see me about?"

Now that he was here, she was quickly losing her nerve. "Oh…I didn't mean you had to rush over."

"That's not how you were acting a few hours ago."

He was right. "I just needed to tell you I've decided against the partnership."

His expression didn't change. "So what made you change your mind?"

She shrugged, unable to look him in the eye. "It's just a lot of work, and we're not sure it will pay off. I'll be taking a big chance. We both would. You should go into business with your uncle."

She was hoping he would get angry and walk out. Instead, he came further into the one-time pantry, which had been converted into an office. "What are you really afraid of, Lace?"

Those dark eyes bored into hers, not letting her hide. "A lot of things, Jeff. Businesses fail all the time. We could lose everything, and I can't afford that. I have my children to think about."

"I thought that was one of the reasons you considered doing the partnership? So your kids would have their mother around, and a chance at a better life."

She didn't have an answer so she shrugged. "I may just sell the ranch altogether."

"The hell you will," he said and took her shoulders. "Tell me the truth, Lacey. Is it me? You afraid I can't pull my weight?"

His strong grip held her close, making it hard for her to think, to talk. "No, Jeff! This has nothing to do with you."

"Then prove it. Trust me to make this work."

"Trust?" she questioned. "I don't know if I can, ever again. Not after what Trevor—" She closed her eyes, hating her weakness.

He released her. "Trevor? What did he do?"

She shook her head. "Nothing that concerns you. I'll deal with it."

Jeff didn't budge, taking up too much space. His scent engulfing her.

"Like you told me this morning," he began. "I'm not leaving until I know you're okay."

When she didn't offer to tell him, he looked over the desk as if he had every right, then picked up the bank notice.

"Give me that," she demanded as she tried to take it away.

His strength won out. Lacey gave up and he read the paper. "How long have you had this?"

She sighed. "It came today."

"Is this why you had the auction?"

Lacey shook her head. "The money that made was for medical bills and the little that left is for the ranch operation. This took me by surprise." She took a breath.

"It seems Trevor took out the loan. He had kept money in an account to make the monthly installments, but there's not enough for the upcoming balloon payment. He never told me," she said in a whisper.

Jeff wanted to believe his friend had a good reason for doing something like this without his wife's knowledge, but it was hard. The problem now was paying it off so she and the kids wouldn't lose anything.

The amount wasn't so large he couldn't handle it himself. He'd saved a lot in the military, but he knew without asking that Lacey wouldn't take his help.

"Let me talk with the bank." He found the name of the guy. "This Mr. Dixon."

"I tried and it didn't do any good."

"If he knows that we're going to partner in a business, maybe he'll agree to more affordable payments spread out over time."

She shook her head. "Jeff, no. This is my problem."

"If we become partners then it's both of ours."

She blinked. "You still want to be my partner?"

Seeing her sadness, his chest tightened. "I wouldn't have asked you if it's not what I wanted." Jeff found himself reaching out and brushing away the moisture from her cheek. "Lace, I'm not going to let you and your kids lose the ranch."

She quickly pulled herself together. "Thank you for that, but there might not be a choice."

"There's always a choice. We just have to come up with a plan."

"How can I?" she asked. "I've already sold most of my stock. My job in town doesn't pay enough to qualify for refinance."

"It's going to be all right, Lace." He couldn't seem

to resist drawing her into his arms. His hand pressed her head against his chest as he absorbed her sadness and fear. "I promise. You're not going to have to move anywhere. We'll find a way to keep the ranch going."

She raised her head. Her eyes filled with tears. She looked beautiful. Without thinking he leaned down and pressed his lips against her forehead. The touch was so fleeting that he didn't think she felt it until she gasped. Her pretty green eyes darkened, but she didn't pull away.

Neither did he. As hard as he tried to think about the loan problem and the future of the ranch, he couldn't. He wasn't able to think at all as he lowered his head and brushed his mouth over hers. She gave a breathy sigh. God help him, he went back for more.

Then he heard, "Hey, Mom."

Jeff jerked back just in time, as Colin poked his head inside the doorway. "I'm hungry."

"So fix yourself a sandwich," Lacey told him.

Colin gave them both another long look, then finally left.

Jeff turned back to Lacey, and seeing her flushed face, guilt once again washed over him. He had no right to kiss her. Not now, not even back then. "I need to go." Grabbing the paper from the desk, he walked out. Even hearing her call his name didn't stop him because if he went back, he'd break all the rules. Again.

Two mornings later, Lacey stood outside the bank in downtown San Angelo. She checked her watch again, knowing she had to be at work in a little over an hour.

Where was Jeff?

She thought back to the other day at the house and

his kiss. She'd been telling herself ever since that it had just been a reassuring kiss. Just a soft brush of his lips over hers. She shivered. The effect had been far more devastating, stirring up feelings she had no business feeling.

She wanted more. What had gotten into her? Not since that summer when she'd broken up with Trevor had she ever thought about another man. Not any man, only Jeff Gentry. And look where that had gotten her.

Well, not this time. She couldn't let this happen. No matter the feelings he'd caused, she wasn't ready. Her life was enough of a mess, and he had his own problems. Adjusting to a new life as well as losing his leg was enough to handle. Not that that bothered her. But they both had too many other complications to deal with.

She closed her eyes. Even now, she still couldn't believe Trevor was gone. He'd been such a big part of her life since adolescence. So had Jeff. Although Trevor had been the one who'd stayed for her. But now, she found herself fantasizing about Jeff.

"Sorry I'm late."

Lacey swung around to see the man in question. "Oh, hi."

Her heart raced as she looked over the handsome man dressed in a white collared shirt, dark trousers and shiny black boots. He was carrying a leather folder.

She groaned. "You look so nice. I should have worn something smarter."

He put on a smile and took her arm. "You look fine. Let's go get that loan."

Inside Mr. Dixon's small office, Jeff tried to relax as the loan officer went over his business proposal.

The young man behind the desk looked as if he was

barely out of college. "This looks very impressive, Mr. Gentry," he said as he sat back in his chair. "On paper. But these are hard times."

Jeff leaned forward. This guy was going to be a hard sell, but he had ten years of military training. "Farmers and ranchers go through rough times, it's a fact of life. I know because my family ranches. And you also know that Mrs. Guthrie's land is worth thirty times the amount of her loan. I'm bringing in stock, and Lacey is going to do the training in this business venture."

"It's still a risk."

"What risk? Our stock combined is worth this much."

Dixon straightened. "Are you willing to put up the horses as collateral?"

"No," Lacey jumped in. "I can't agree to that."

Jeff didn't know much about loans, but shouldn't the land be enough? "It'll be okay, Lace." He turned back to Dixon. "I need to make a quick call." He stood and moved across the room, punching in numbers.

His uncle answered. "Chance Randell."

Jeff explained to him what was going on. Chance listened then asked to give him ten minutes and he'd get back to him.

Mr. Dixon reluctantly granted them the time, then he called to get some coffee. Soon a secretary came in, along with another man.

Mr. Dixon stood immediately. "Mr. Handley," he greeted the visitor eagerly.

The older gentleman ignored the loan officer and walked directly to Lacey and Jeff. "Hello, I'm Bert Handley, the bank manager. You must be Mrs. Guthrie and Mr. Gentry."

"Yes, sir, we are," Jeff said.

Mr. Handley turned to Lacey. "I'm sorry to hear about the loss of your husband, Mrs. Guthrie. I wish we had known sooner."

"Thank you, Mr. Handley," Lacey said. "That's why we're here. Since my husband's death, I can't handle the terms of the loan."

The bank manager smiled. "Then we'd best work something out."

"We've been working on that, Mr. Handley," Dixon said quickly. "They're going to put up their stock as collateral."

Bert Handley walked behind the desk and glanced over the loan papers. The older man frowned. "I don't see a reason why the ranch itself can't be enough to secure a loan."

Dixon was nervous. "It's just that with a new business venture and no assured income, I thought—"

Handley shook his head as he turned the page. "With these excellent credit scores, surely we can come up with a better interest rate." He glanced at Dixon. "Larry, why don't I take care of this? I've been a friend of the family for years." He smiled at Jeff. "I gave Chance Randell his first loan."

At the mention of the well-known Randell name, Dixon excused himself and left the room.

Handley looked back and forth between the two. "I like to think we're still a neighborhood bank. Since the circumstances with your husband have changed, I'm sure we can also adjust the terms of the loan with a better interest rate for the two of you."

"No, Mr. Handley. This is my debt and I don't want Mr. Gentry liable for any of it."

The man looked over his reading glasses. "This is a business loan, Mrs. Guthrie. I need both your names on it and both of you are to be responsible for it."

Jeff felt Lacey tense. "Would you excuse us a moment?" At the man's nod, he took Lacey outside the small office and into the hall. "You can pay the money, I don't care, Lace, but we need to get the loan first."

She crossed her arms over her chest. "I won't have you take care of this for me, Jeff."

"Okay, what do we do? Walk away? You lose the ranch and move into town?"

He saw the determination on her face. "No. I plan to sell you the cabin and the acreage around it."

Jeff didn't even need to think about it. "Fine, when we're rich and famous, I'll sell it back to you. That section of land is valuable and the cabin belongs to Colin."

She nodded. "Thank you."

"Don't thank me yet, we could still lose our shirts."

She smiled. "Now I feel like we're equal partners."

And suddenly he was a landowner. "Then let's go have Mr. Handley draw up the papers."

CHAPTER SEVEN

THAT evening, Lacey arrived home from work with the kids in tow to find Jeff on the porch. She was tired and still in her uniform when she came up the steps.

"Hi, Jeff," Emily greeted him, her blue eyes lit up with excitement. "What are you doing here? It's dark outside and the horses are sleeping."

He leaned down to her. "I know. I just need to talk to your mother for a few minutes."

"Okay." She looked to her mother. "Mom, he needs to talk to you."

Lacey didn't want to talk to anyone. All she wanted was a long hot bath, a glass of wine and no interruptions. But it didn't look like that would happen. "Give me a minute.

"Colin, take your sister upstairs and start her bath. And don't leave the water running this time."

Her son grumbled something, but then looked at Jeff. "Okay, Mom." He took Emily's hand and they disappeared inside.

She turned to Jeff. "Was there something else we need to talk about?"

"If you have a few minutes. We were so rushed this

morning. I wanted to make sure you're okay with everything."

"Come in." She went inside, leading him through the kitchen and pantry, then into the small office.

She turned and faced Jeff. He looked freshly showered and shaved with a crisply starched Western shirt and jeans. Maybe he was going out.

He pulled a paper from his back pocket. "I spoke with my dad's lawyer after you went to work and he came up with an agreement for us. If you want you can have your attorney go over it." He frowned at her. "I figured that everything would be fifty-fifty. I own stock; you have the stables and the experience for training."

"You now own part of the ranch." She hated giving that up or anything that actually threatened her kids' future.

"Temporarily. Until the loan is paid off."

She looked down at the papers. She also didn't have an attorney. "Can you give me a few days to look it over?"

"Sure." He hesitated. "Lacey, we don't have to go through with this. I don't want your land. I'm fine with investing in the business without it."

His dark gaze held hers. She felt a rush go through her, making it hard to concentrate. "I know, but I can't let you take all the risk."

He smiled at her and her heart tripped.

"I don't think this is a risk at all. Our stock is top-rate. It will be slow going at first, but once we start advertising about your training, things will pick up."

She still wasn't sure that would mean anything to anyone.

"We should come up with a name," he suggested. "I thought we could use our initials. G&G Quarter Horses. Lacey Guthrie, trainer."

She suddenly felt more of Trevor fading from her life and Jeff intruding in it. "The name will change?"

He paused. "Not the ranch, just the business. Maybe both our names could help us, with my dad and uncle in rough-stock business. The Gentry name is pretty well known."

He was right, she thought.

"Don't forget we have Chance Randell as our pitchman. And if we get a few more boarders we can hire that stablehand we talked about."

Her head was spinning. "You've been thinking about this a lot."

"Just since we talked to Mr. Handley." He grinned. "This is going to work, Lace. Our partnership."

She couldn't help but get caught up in his excitement. "You make me want to believe it."

"Believe it. This is your future, too." He checked his watch. "I wish we had more time to talk, but I have to go."

Why did it bother her that he seemed anxious to leave? "You have a hot date?" she blurted out. Oh, no, she sounded so desperate.

Jeff looked confused at her question. "I'm meeting Brandon, Jay and my brother, Drew." He sighed. "They talked me into going out for a drink. It's kind of a welcome-home celebration. I'm meeting them at a place called the Horseman's Club."

It was an upscale country-western bar, also known as the best hook-up place in the area. "That should be nice."

"I'll let you know tomorrow," he said. "I'm not much for big crowds, drinking or dancing."

What about pretty women in tight jeans with the big...buckles? she wanted to scream. "Well, I won't hold you up." She headed to the door. "I guess I'll see you tomorrow, just not so early."

Jeff stopped. "I'll be here at my usual time. Chance is coming by, he wants to talk to us about which stallion would be best to cover Bonnie."

"So soon?"

He shifted his hat in his hands. "Is there any reason to wait?"

"No, I guess not," Lacey agreed, once again feeling the excitement. They were truly going to be partners. Why was that bothering her so much? *Because Jeff Gentry would be a part of her life.*

Two hours later, the cousins sat at a corner table in the large bar as a Kenny Chesney song played in the background. For a weeknight, the place was crowded with people. His single brother, Drew, and Brandon's younger brother, Jay, were taking advantage of the abundance of girls and were out on the dance floor.

Jeff took a sip of the beer he'd been nursing the past hour, then looked across the table at Brandon drinking cola. He was the designated driver.

"You're not having much fun, are you?" his cousin asked.

"It's not bad. I've just never been big on the club scene."

"Do you think I picked this place?" His cousin smiled as he nodded toward the dance floor. "Blame it on Drew and Jay. It was their idea. Nora wasn't exactly crazy about it, either. Not that she has anything to worry about."

Jeff envied Brandon. The man had found love with someone special and his life seemed to be going great. He thought about Lacey. He would rather be with her, going over some ideas for the business. A few nights ago he hadn't been thinking about business when he'd held her close, when he'd kissed her. Those feelings hadn't changed over the years.

"Hey, how's the new partnership going?" Brandon asked, drawing Jeff back to the present.

He nodded. "Good. Uncle Chance has agreed to help out."

Grinning, his cousin shook his head. "You've been in the military so long, I didn't think you'd ever come home. Now, you're a horse-breeder."

Home. It had been a while since Jeff had thought about San Angelo as home. Nor had he thought he'd end up partners with his best friend's widow. "I didn't have much choice. I was forced into finding a new career." He found himself smiling, too. "But so far I'm enjoying it."

"And a pretty woman doesn't hurt, either."

Jeff shook his head. "There's nothing going on between Lacey and me," he said, knowing he wouldn't go there again.

Brandon grinned. "If you say so. Just so you know, there's plenty of room in Mustang Valley for another Randell."

"Yeah, this family has changed so much, and you're the first of our generation to get married. You have a son, too."

Brandon leaned forward and lowered his voice.

"And there'll be another Randell soon. We're not saying anything yet, but Nora's pregnant."

A pang of jealousy hit Jeff, surprising him. "That's great news." For a split second, he let himself think about the possibility of having his own wife and child. Lacey immediately came to mind, but he quickly pushed aside the fleeting dream.

"Keep it quiet for a while. We haven't told Mom and Dad yet."

"You can trust me, I only give my name, rank and serial number," Jeff said wryly.

They were both laughing when their younger brothers returned. "Hey, what's so funny?" Drew asked.

Brandon shook his head. "It's a private joke."

Drew pulled out his chair and sat down. In his early twenties, Andrew resembled Wyatt with his dark hair, but he had lighter eyes like their mom. "Well, here's something that's not so private. Granddad Hank's cattle drive." Drew looked at his older brother. "And he's insisting that Jeff's going to be the trail boss."

Jeff shifted in his chair. "A couple of weeks back, he mentioned something about it, but I didn't think anything had been finalized yet."

This time it was Jay who spoke up. "Oh, no, you know Granddad. He has it all planned out. He's even had Aunt Josie put it up on the Web site, advertising it for Labor Day weekend. The first Annual Randell Ranch Cattle Drive. Seems there's a lot of interest, too. One thing I know for sure, Hank wants this to be headed by the grandkids. He said he wants the next generation of Randells to show what they're made of."

Brandon smiled. "I believe Hank's just thrown out

a challenge. Sounds like fun. What about you, Jeff, you planning on going?"

"I haven't told Hank one way or the other." He wasn't sure if he could do it, but the idea sounded intriguing. He was interested in finding out more details. "I'm not sure I'm in shape for it."

"Then get in shape," his brother told him. "Put in some time on horseback. We've got some fence you can ride."

Jay glanced at his brother Brandon. "You probably could use the exercise, too."

Brandon pulled in his flat stomach. "What do you mean? I'm in great shape." He looked at Jeff. "We've got about five weeks to pull this together. You can come by the ranch on my days off. We'll chase some cows around."

The younger brothers broke up with laughter. "I can't wait to see this," Jay said.

Jeff suddenly felt the stirring of competition. He found he liked that. "Cuz," he said to Brandon, "looks like we have to show these two how it's done. If you can spare a few dozen steers and bring them up to the cabin, we can hone our skills. There's plenty of grass and water to keep them happy."

"You're telling me," Jay said. "The Guthrie place has the best underground spring in the area. If Lacey ever wants to sell us some water, we'd be interested in buying. In fact I would love to have that acreage to run my own herd."

Jeff had never paid much attention to the water shortage, but that could be another source of income. "If and when you're serious I'll talk it over with Lacey."

Jay grinned. "Man, oh, man, you're home less than a month and you've bought a couple of quality quarter horses and got a pretty partner, to boot. How did you get so lucky?"

A few weeks ago, Jeff hadn't felt so lucky, but things were starting to look better. He thought about Lacey again. No, a *lot* better.

There was a tap on his shoulder and Jeff turned to find a pretty brunette. She was very young, and decked out in tight jeans and a fitted Western shirt. "You want to dance, cowboy?"

Jeff held his panic in check. He'd never been the best dancer to begin with, but now...he wasn't sure if he could do this.

Before he could answer, his brother spoke up. "Why would you want to dance with this old guy?" Drew stood. "I'm younger and much better-looking." He took the young girl's hand and tugged her toward the dance floor. She didn't look as if she were disappointed at all with the switch. When the music changed to a ballad, Jay got up and snagged a partner, leaving Brandon and Jeff alone once more.

Brandon leaned forward. "She was a little on the young side. But it's nice to know you can still attract them." He shrugged. "Of course, it's not the same if it's not the right woman."

Jeff recalled his kiss with Lacey and his body stirred to life. She'd always had that effect on him. Hell, he was crazy about her; that hadn't changed since the day they'd met.

Jeff looked at his cousin. There was no use lying about it. "There's only been one woman for me."

Brandon nodded, knowing who he was talking about. "Then don't you think it's about time you went after her?"

* * *

The next morning, Chance Randell arrived at the Guthrie place. Nervous, Lacey climbed off Fancy as Jeff walked into the corral with his uncle. She'd never officially met Chance, only heard about him from Jeff and, of course, from quarter-horse circles. She wiped her forehead on her sleeve and went to greet them.

"Lacey, this is my Uncle Chance."

"It's a pleasure to meet you, Mr. Randell."

The handsome older man took her outstretched hand and shook it firmly. "Please, it's Chance. May I call you Lacey?"

"Of course." She glanced at Jeff, then back to his uncle. "Jeff said you're interested in Rebel."

Chance nodded, but his attention was on the liver-chestnut filly. "Of course, my wife threatened to leave me if I brought home another horse. So I'm glad Jeff got them."

Lacey smiled. "And I'm happy that saved your marriage."

He winked at her. "It wouldn't be the first time I've been sent to the barn over the years." His expert eye and hands moved over the filly, letting out a soft whistle. "She's a beauty."

Jeff smiled. "I'm trying to convince Lacey to train her seriously. To get her name out there."

"Are you training her?" Chance asked.

Lacey nodded. "Last year, Trevor and I entered Fancy in a local reining competition, but I haven't had much time for training lately."

"That's all changed since the partnership," Jeff began. "You should see these two working together."

"It's not my expertise," Chance said and turned to

Jeff. "That would be Tess's area, but I bet she wouldn't mind stopping by to have a look."

"I might ask her," Jeff agreed.

Chance nodded. "So let's see this stallion I've heard so much about."

They walked into the barn. Lacey stayed back, but Chance refused to let her lag behind, asking her questions about the layout of the place and complimenting her on the operation. After all the work she and Trevor had put in, that made her feel good.

They reached Rebel's stall and the stallion whinnied in excitement. Chance immediately went inside. With Lacey's coaxing, the horse allowed the older Randell to look him over.

"You say Bonnie is Rebel's dam?"

"Yes," Lacey answered. "He's a two-year-old, sired by Johnny Reb."

"He's a good-looking horse. Your husband knew what he was doing." Chance looked at her. "I'm sorry to bring up your recent loss."

"Not a problem. My husband would have liked you saying how much you're impressed with his horses." She wasn't sad at the mention of Trevor's name. He'd left a legacy in his horses. "I think the best way to honor him is to keep this bloodline going."

Chance nodded. "Then if it's all right with you, I want to bring Rebel to my place and introduce him to two of my mares. I prefer to do live cover, but if there's any risk of injury to the stallion, we'll go AI. My foreman, Terry Hansen, handles most of the breeding and he takes all the precautions, and I'll be there, too. But it's up to you."

"I don't have a problem with it." Lacey looked at Jeff. "What do you think?"

"I think we should pack Rebel up and go introduce him to the ladies."

Later that day, Jeff had Rebel loaded in the trailer and headed to the Randell Quarter Horse Ranch. He wasn't surprised that Lacey wanted to come along. After all, they needed to decide on the stallion they wanted to breed with Bonnie.

With the kids off with the babysitter, it felt strange to have Lacey to himself. Not that it mattered, there wasn't anything going on between them but their connection to the business. He thought back to their kiss. Could he even classify what had happened between them as a kiss? A simple brush of his mouth against hers. It was enough to remind him of years ago, and that one stolen afternoon. Only he'd be crazy to think about getting another chance with her. His hand rubbed his thigh, quickly reminding him of his limitation.

What he needed to do was help plan her and the kids' future. He stole a glance across the cab to watch the quiet woman leaning against the headrest, her eyes closed. She looked tired, but it didn't take away from her beauty or the fact that he couldn't stop desiring her.

His gaze darted back to the road. "Something wrong?"

She sighed. "I don't like to leave Colin and Emily. I spend too much time away at work as it is."

"Colin and Emily could have come along. They both know how to act around horses." He meant it. They were good kids.

She shook her head. "This is business, Jeff, so I

prefer to treat it professionally. Besides, I'll be busy getting Rebel settled. That might not be an easy job. He hasn't been out of his barn before. You saw how he fought getting into the trailer."

Jeff turned off the highway. "So you're along to mother him?"

She tried not to smile. "This is his first time."

Jeff pulled the truck up beside the barn. "Don't worry, it'll come natural to him."

There was a playful expression on her face. "You mean what comes natural to all males?"

He turned in time to see her pink face before she quickly climbed out of the cab. Had she been thinking about their one time together as well?

He shut off the engine and got out, too. They met at the back of the trailer. He pulled his hat down to shield his face from the sunlight.

She was working the gate when he stopped her. "I'll do it," he told her. "I can handle the heavy stuff."

Lacey stood back as he dropped the ramp. "I should bring him out." Anything to put some space between her and Jeff. She couldn't think about him as a man. Yeah, right. Jeff Gentry was definitely a hundred-percent male.

She touched Rebel's rump then ran a soothing hand along his flank, whispering reassuring words. She took hold of his lead rope and coaxed him to back up, aware of the narrow ramp, but Jeff was there guiding her.

Rebel was finally out and definitely excited about his new surroundings. She held him securely, but the mare at a nearby corral was calling to him. The stallion showed evidence that he was very interested in the attention.

It took the two of them and a stable hand to get Rebel into a separate barn and stall. Before Jeff could get out of the way, the horse had kicked him. He cursed several times and limped out.

Lacey went to him. "I should have warned you about him. Did he hurt you?"

He grimaced in pain. "I'll live," he said, rubbing his leg. "Wouldn't you know it, he got my one good leg!"

CHAPTER EIGHT

GETTING kicked by a horse wasn't funny, and Jeff wasn't laughing. It had really hurt, but he hadn't been going to drop his jeans to show everyone the bruise. Now there wasn't a choice as he lay on the examining table in the emergency room two hours later. His leg was throbbing like crazy. What worried him was the horse's hoof had caught him right above the knee. What riled him the most was that he hadn't been able to move fast enough to get out of the way.

"I said I was fine," he told Lacey, looking at his uncle for support. Chance's expression told him he wasn't getting any.

"Hey, I've been kicked a hundred times," Chance said. "It's nothing to mess with."

Lacey folded her arms. "Maybe if you'd gotten kicked in your hard head, we wouldn't have to be here at all."

"Very funny," Jeff said, seeing the worry on her face. "I'm fine." He turned to his uncle. "So don't call Mom or Dad. I don't want them to worry over nothing." He'd hate for them to go through that pain again.

Chance agreed. "Then stop complaining and let the doctor look at you."

Jeff sighed and relented. “Okay. Now, will you two stop hovering? I can handle this myself.”

Before they could argue the point, the doctor came in, carrying his chart. “Mr. Gentry?”

“Yes, that’s me.”

“I’m Doctor Stoner.” He shook Jeff’s hand, then glanced at the chart. “So you were kicked by a horse?” Without waiting for an answer, he turned to Lacey. “Are you Mrs. Gentry?”

Lacey blinked. “No, I’m a…friend. His uncle and I brought him in.”

“It’s always good to be cautious in these matters. I should examine the patient, so I’ll have to ask you both to leave.”

“Of course.” Lacey glanced over her shoulder at Jeff as she went to the door. “We’ll be outside,” she told him.

He waved them away. “I’ll be sure to holler if I need anything.” He wasn’t willing to strip down in front of Lacey. Not that he hadn’t dreamed of it for years, but not like this. Not with only one leg. Nope, those dreams had long since died.

For the next thirty minutes, Lacey paced in the waiting area while Chance sat in one of the many plastic chairs, pretending to read a discarded newspaper.

“Do you think you should call his parents?” she asked, wondering what was taking so long.

He shook his head. “That’s up to Jeff. He’ll call them if it’s anything serious.”

“Do you think it is?”

Chance shrugged. “It’s a pretty deep bruise. I don’t think anything is broken, but that’s why we’re here, to find out.”

She nodded, wishing his reassurance would calm her. "I'm worried there might be some damage to his knee. I don't know much about the situation with the leg he lost, but doesn't he need his good one? I mean, both his legs are good, of course, it's just..." She only knew what Jeff had told Colin the night he'd found her son. That he'd lost part of his calf and his foot.

"Lacey, let's not borrow trouble. Jeff was able to walk in here and he'll probably walk out of here with two good knees."

"He was limping pretty badly."

"He favored it a bit," Chance corrected.

"I never should have let him handle Rebel."

Chance stood and walked to her. "That stallion is his horse. More importantly, Jeff needs to handle things on his own. I think the last thing he wants is to be treated like an invalid. He's gone through a lot and he's already come so far." He raised an eyebrow. "If you care about him as much as I think you do, don't let him see your worry. He might mistake it for doubt."

She gasped. "I don't doubt him."

Chance winked. "Good, because I don't think my nephew thinks of you as a mother."

She couldn't stop her blush. "It doesn't keep me from worrying about him."

"Of course not, we all do. Trouble is, Jeff spent the last ten years in the army doing heroic things. That all ended when he lost his leg. Although we think he's no less of a man, he needs to prove it to himself."

A pretty redheaded nurse walked toward them. Smiling, Chance went to greet her and pulled her into a tight embrace. "How's my pretty niece?"

"I'd be fine, if I could keep you Randells out of the

ER." She looked at Lacey. "Hi, you must be Lacey Guthrie, I'm Brandon's wife, Nora. It's nice to finally meet you. Only I'm sorry it's here."

Lacey smiled. "It's nice to meet you, too. How's Jeff?"

"Being just as disagreeable as the rest of the Randells who've been patients here. He's fine, though, and very lucky there wasn't any damage to his knee. The doctor will have instructions and medication for him." She frowned, then lowered her voice. "I doubt it's a good idea for Jeff to stay alone up at the cabin."

Chance nodded. "Not a problem, but I might need Brandon's help with this."

"That can be arranged if needed." Nora laughed. "Jeff should be dressed now." She turned to Lacey. "Once he's feeling better, I hope you both will come to the house for dinner, and bring your kids."

Lacey nodded. She liked Nora. "Thank you. That would be nice."

Nora hugged Chance once again and walked off, then returned pushing Jeff out in a wheelchair. He didn't look happy.

"Can we get out of here?" he grumbled.

"Should I take you home with me, or to your parents?" Chance asked.

"Neither, to the cabin," he said.

His uncle shook his head. "That's not an option."

"I'm not going to Mom and Dad's place. I only have to stay off my leg for a few days. I can handle that on my own."

Lacey watched the two Randell men glare at each other and she found herself speaking up. "You can stay with me."

* * *

Twenty-four hours later, Lacey knew one thing for sure. Jeff Gentry was the worst patient ever. He had rejected any and all help from her.

Of course, the drugs had him sleeping a lot. That was definitely a good thing. Chance had gone to get some clothes from the cabin and brought them by. Jeff had moved into the small sewing room at the end of the hall upstairs. There was only a pull-out sofa, but he said it was fine. She'd also stayed home from work the previous night thinking he'd need her. He hadn't.

After supper, her kids went to watch some television while she fixed a supper plate for the patient. Jeff needed to eat. Taking pills on an empty stomach wasn't a good thing. She set a slice of meat loaf and a baked potato on the tray, added a roll and some iced tea, then carried it up the wide staircase to Jeff's room.

The fourth and seventh steps creaked. That was just one of the many repairs that needed to be made in the century-old house. But in spite of it being overdue for a fresh coat of paint and the plumbing rattling, she loved the place.

Lacey made her way down the long hall and heard voices. At first she thought it was the TV but soon realized it was her daughter. She stopped outside Jeff's bedroom.

"See, my dolly has an owie on her knee, too. Does yours hurt really, really bad?"

Jeff had never had anything against kids, but he wanted to be alone to wallow in his own misery. "Not much," he answered.

"Did they put a big Band-Aid on it?" she asked. "Mommy has kitty cat Band-Aids if you want one."

He nearly smiled. Okay, so she was cute. "That's all right, thanks. I'm good."

"'Kay." She nodded. "I'm sorry Rebel kicked you." She shook her head, sending her ponytail swinging back and forth. "He didn't mean to. I think he got scared 'cause he had to go away. I get scared sometimes when I have to leave my mommy. Do you get scared?"

Those big blue eyes studied him. "Sometimes."

"My daddy got scared." She swallowed. "When he was sick, he cried 'cause he was going to miss me, Mommy and Colin. He went away to heaven." She blinked back tears. "I miss him."

He felt his chest tighten painfully. "We all do, sweetie." He reached out and touched her arm. That must have been an invitation because the next thing he knew the tiny girl was curled up against him, clutching her doll. He found all he could do was wrap his arms around her small frame.

"Shh, Emily. It's okay." His voice was rough with emotion. "I know your daddy wouldn't want you to be sad. He would want you to be happy."

She looked up and wiped her eyes. "That's what Mommy says. But sometimes I get sad."

"Well, you come to me and I'll tell you some funny stories about your daddy and you'll laugh."

He needed to remember those good times, too. "Really?"

"Really."

Jeff glanced at the doorway and saw Lacey watching them. Great. How long had she been there? By the look on her face, she'd heard it all.

"I thought you might be hungry," she said, and carried the tray inside. "Emily, weren't you watching your favorite show?"

"I want to talk to Jeff. He's going to tell me stories about Daddy. He says I'll laugh so much that I won't think about being sad."

"Well, if anyone knows stories, it's Jeff. But I think it's time to say goodnight."

In a flash those tiny arms wrapped about his neck and she kissed his cheek. "Goodnight, Jeff." Her warm breath brushed his face, making him realize all that he had missed being a soldier. "Happy dreams. That's what my daddy used to say."

"'Night, sweetie. Happy dreams to you, too."

"I'll be in your room in a bit, Emily," Lacey said to her daughter. "So get into bed."

She put the tray on the desk and went to straighten the blanket over Jeff. He hated her fussing, even though he knew it was ungrateful of him. "You don't have to do this, Lacey."

"I only brought you supper."

He sighed. "Go to your daughter."

Those green eyes met his as she leaned in close. "Do you need anything before I go?"

He could think of a million things he wanted from her. He shook his head. "I'll probably sleep," he lied.

She glanced down at his jeans. "You should take off your pants, you'd be more comfortable."

Yeah, that would do the trick. "I'm fine, Lacey. Now, go."

"Okay, Mr. Tough Guy." She brought the food tray to the bed, tossed him a grin, then walked out. When the door closed, he released a long breath. He wasn't going to survive this. He popped a pill into his mouth and took a hearty drink of water, hoping he'd be able to sleep. More importantly, that he wouldn't dream of Lacey.

* * *

Hours later, Lacey jerked awake and sat up in bed. She'd heard a noise. In the pitch-blackness, she pulled back the sheet and got up. Since Trevor's death, she'd left her bedroom door open, wanting to be able to hear the kids if they needed her.

She checked their rooms, but both Colin and Emily were sound asleep. She glanced at the door at the end of the hall. No, she wasn't about to disturb him. Before she was able to turn to go back to her bed she heard the sound again. It was coming from Jeff's room.

Without hesitation she opened the door, allowing the hall light to illuminate the bed where he was thrashing around in the tangled sheets. He cried out again. She went to his side and called his name. She gripped his arm and immediately felt the sweat. "Jeff, wake up."

He tried to push her away. "No, don't." His expression was a grimace.

"Jeff, you're dreaming. Wake up," she called, but finished with a gasp as he grabbed her and pinned her down on the mattress.

He leaned over her, breathing hard. In the shadowy darkness, he looked disorientated as he tried to focus. "Lace? Oh, God. What happened?"

Too aware of his body on hers, she was suddenly breathless. "You cried out. I thought you were in pain."

"You have no idea."

She shivered. "Are you okay, can I get you anything?"

"Many things," he told her. "But I don't think you want to hear what they are." He finally rolled off her and dropped back onto the pillow. "Go back to bed, Lace. I'm not in the mood to talk."

She missed the feel of him. What was wrong with her,

that she couldn't resist this man? "Were you having a nightmare?"

Although she wasn't touching him, she felt him tense and sat up. "Was it about the accident?"

"First of all," he began, "it wasn't an accident. It was the enemy's job to kill me. Just like it was mine to do everything possible to get them first." There was a long pause. "I lost."

"That's not true. I hear you saved the lives of several men."

"So my uncle has been doing some talking. I was in the army, Lacey, I was doing my job. What I'd been trained to do."

"Don't you dare make it sound like it was nothing, Jeff Gentry." She felt as though she was on a soapbox. "You went in under heavy fire to get those men out of harm's way."

His head snapped around to her. "In the end, they had to carry *me* out."

"And you all made it out alive. You have to look at the positive, Jeff. You came home alive. You may have lost part of your leg, but for those of us who care about you, what's important is that you're still around." She couldn't help but think about Trevor. "I think you were pretty lucky."

When he didn't say anything, she started to stand. "What's the use? You're not going to believe me, and I don't have to listen to your self-pity."

He grabbed her arm and stopped her from leaving. "Don't go, Lace."

The gentleness of his touch surprised her. "Why shouldn't I? Everything I say is wrong."

"It's not. It's just being in the hospital today brought back bad memories."

"I understand that, Jeff, but don't turn on your friends. I'm just trying to help." She saw his sweat-stained T-shirt outlining his muscular chest. She was tempted to put her palm against his skin, wanting a connection with him again.

"I know it doesn't seem like it, but I appreciate it."

She got up and went to his duffel bag. She pulled out a pair of sweatpants and a T-shirt. "You should change out of your clothes and try and get some sleep."

"I'm not one of your kids, Lace," he said.

"Then stop acting like one." She tossed the shirt at him.

He cursed as he fought with the damp T-shirt but managed to get it off. She couldn't help but study the impressive body, the toned arms and chest, the flat stomach. A lot different from the young boy she once knew.

He caught her surveillance of his semi-naked body. "Shouldn't I get to return the favor?"

She was shocked at his words, then suddenly realized she was only wearing a pair of boxer shorts and a tank top. "Sorry, I just ran in here when you called out."

"No need to apologize."

Jeff shifted in the bed, knowing he had to be crazy not to get her out of here. He'd been working so hard to resist her that he'd used up all his energy, and yet he still wanted her. And now he had no fight left.

"You should have gotten out of your clothes earlier," she said, her voice a shaky whisper. "I mean, sleeping in jeans can't be comfortable."

"I didn't need to take them off."

Her hair caught against her cheek as she glanced away.

Jeff reached out and drew her back down on the bed.

His pulse raced out of control as he cupped the back of her neck. In the shadowed light he watched her eyes widen, but when she didn't resist, he gave a gentle tug.

His lips brushed over hers and she gasped, but didn't pull away. He took it as a go, and closed his mouth over hers. His lungs tightened as he fought to breathe, but who needed air anyway? He deepened the kiss as he pulled her close, crushing her against his chest. His long wait was finally over; Lacey was in his arms at last.

With soft whimpering sounds, her lips parted and he swept his tongue inside, tasting her sweetness. Her hands went around his neck and she clung to him as they drank from each other.

He broke off the kiss, but went to work on her neck, feeling her shivers. He raised his head and looked down at her. "Tell me to stop, Lace."

She opened her mouth and hesitated, then finally said, "I can't." Her breath rushed out as she lifted up and placed her mouth against his.

He swiftly shifted the position as he rolled his body over hers. She moved under him, causing him to groan.

"Damn it, woman. You're not making this easy."

"Jeff," she gasped as she pushed him onto his back and began kissing him. He enjoyed the assault until she started to unfasten his belt.

He finally came to his senses and broke off the kiss. He pressed his head against her forehead, feeling their hearts pounding in unison.

"We can't do this again," he said, somehow finding the breath to speak.

Jeff rolled away and sat up. What was he thinking? He couldn't make love to Lacey. He couldn't let her see him this way.

"Jeff." She touched his back. "If it's because of your leg…it doesn't make any difference to me."

He nearly jackknifed off the bed. "I don't want to talk about this, Lace."

She didn't move. He had to get rid of her, whatever it took.

"Of course, what do you expect when you come into a man's bedroom in the middle of the night?"

She blinked at his cruel words, but it worked. She got up. "Go to hell, Gentry." The door slammed behind her as she left.

"I'm in it right now," he whispered to the empty room.

CHAPTER NINE

THE next morning, right after breakfast, Lacey gathered the kids and went to work in the barn. Colin and Emily cleaned out the stalls and fed the horses, with the promise that she'd take them riding later.

As hard and as long as she'd worked, it couldn't erase what had happened with Jeff last night. Good Lord, what had possessed her? First of all, she had no business being in his room in the middle of the night. Definitely, she shouldn't have gotten into the position of ending up in bed with him. She closed her eyes a moment, recalling years ago when Jeff had rejected her the first time.

You'd think she'd learn her lesson.

She straightened and began to smooth the straw. Well, it wasn't going to happen again. Getting Gentry out of her house was going to be her main goal.

Coming out of Fancy's stall, Lacey saw Hank Barrett walk down the aisle toward her. He was probably here to see his grandson. Good. Maybe he'd take Jeff home with him.

Hank smiled as he tipped his hat. "Mornin', Lacey."

"Hello, Hank."

"I'm sorry to come calling so early, but I hear Jeff got a little too close to his new stallion yesterday."

"He did, but he won't be happy that you heard about the accident."

Hank shook his head. "It's amazing how much pride a man's got, isn't it? And the Randell men seem to have more than most."

How true. "Would you believe he's been the perfect houseguest?"

They both laughed and it felt good to Lacey.

"That's not the intense young man I remember." He sobered. "Years in the military have had a lot to do with that. It's hard to accept change sometimes. I'm hoping I can help."

"Well, you're welcome to try. Jeff is upstairs in the room at the end of the hall."

Hank started to walk off, then stopped. "If I haven't said it before, thank you for all you're doing for him."

"We're partners, and friends." The last part was what she needed to concentrate on, and nothing more. It was getting harder and harder, not because she didn't like him, but because she was beginning to care too much.

Jeff was tired of lying around, but he had to agree with the doctor, it had helped the swelling go down on his knee. It was feeling much better today, yet, he wasn't sure he could handle even one more night here. Not with Lacey playing nurse. No matter what, he was headed back to the cabin tomorrow. At least there he would have some privacy.

Although no one had come to see him this morning. Only Colin, when he'd brought breakfast. Since he'd wakened, he managed to make it to the bathroom for a shower, but on coming out he'd noticed the house was silent.

Good. Dressed in a pair of sweats, he'd removed his prosthesis and was able to relax on the bed. He leaned back and closed his eyes, but memories of last night came flooding back. Kissing Lacey, and feeling the softness of her body pressed against him. The way she'd put her hands on him, eager to please.

He shifted on the bed. What if he hadn't stopped her? He didn't want to see her reaction when she saw what was left of his leg. He didn't know if he could handle that.

There was a knock on the door, and he tossed the sheet over his legs. "Come in."

Hank peered in and smiled. "I hear you tangled with a stallion."

"Hi, Granddad. Uncle Chance told you, didn't he?"

Hank shook his head. "It was Nora. But you should have let your parents know."

"It's nothing. I got bruised."

"That's what Nora said. And that you needed to stay off of it for a few days."

"Which means my time will be up tomorrow and I'll be gone. So there isn't anything to worry about."

"Did I say I was worried? I needed to talk to you, that's all."

"Have a seat."

Hank pulled a chair over to the bed. "I came to see if you've given any more thought to the cattle drive? I still want you to head it up."

Jeff still had doubts. "Wouldn't Jay or Drew be better?"

"With your background, I believe you can keep

everyone in line. And believe me, your cousins can get out of hand real fast. I want one person in charge. You."

He felt honored. "I haven't herded cattle in a long time."

"So? You'll have several men helping to do that. We already have twenty-six want-to-be-wranglers signed up and paying for this experience. I've assembled a team of the cousins. The next generation of Randells, including your brother, Drew, and your sister, Kelly. There's at least a dozen."

"It sounds tempting," Jeff told him. "I haven't spent any length of time in the saddle in years."

"You have time to get in shape."

"I'll never be in perfect shape again, Hank."

"Yes, you will. In fact, right now, you're in better shape than most. Jeff, you're the boy who overcame an abusive father. And the man who always strived for perfection. None of us are perfect, son. We're only human." Hank laid his hand on Jeff's stump. "You have to accept this, but it's not all that you are. If you believe anything, believe this. You are the man you always were, because that comes from within here. Your heart." Hank's work-roughened fingers touched his chest. "Please, don't let what happened to you change that."

Jeff swallowed. "I'll try not to."

Hank nodded. "Good. You'll be my trail boss, then?"

It was hard to say no to this man. "Yes, sir."

His grandfather grinned. "That's what I like, a man who shows respect to his elders."

There was a knock on the door, and Emily peeked inside and gave them her best smile. "Hi, Jeff. Hi, Mr.

Hank." She strolled in. Today she was dressed in jeans and a T-shirt that looked pretty dirty. "Did you come over to see Jeff's owie?" she asked Hank.

"Yes, I did, and to ask him to help with a cattle drive."

Another head poked through the door. Colin. "A cattle drive! Who's going on a cattle drive?"

Hank looked from the children to Jeff. "You know, Brandon is bringing Zach along. Colin's about the same age."

"Would you like to go?" Hank asked.

The boy's eyes lit up. "Wow! A real cattle drive. Could I?"

"You need to ask your mother," Jeff quickly added, not sure that Lacey wanted anything to do with him after last night.

The door opened wider and Lacey came in. "Ask me what?"

Jeff hadn't seen her since the night before, and he found his hunger for her hadn't diminished any. She had on her standard work jeans and an unbuttoned blouse over a tank top. Most of her hair had come loose from her ponytail, yet she looked sexy and capable.

Hank handled the explanation. "We're talking about the cattle drive."

Lacey didn't know what was going on. She'd come up to invite Hank to stay for lunch, but she hadn't expected to find a party going on in Jeff's room. She couldn't help but notice that, although Jeff had the sheet covering his legs, he wasn't wearing his prosthesis. Trying not to seem too inquisitive, she saw that he still had a lot of his leg. She glanced at his face, their gazes held, and she tried to relay to him that she didn't think of him any differently.

Hank once again broke into her thoughts. "I just had a thought," he said. "Lacey, can you cook?"

"She's great," Colin chimed in. "She can cook everything. Beef stew is my favorite."

She shook her head, coming back to the present. "Well, we're not having stew for lunch," she told her son. "But you're welcome to stay, Hank."

The older man's face lit up in a big grin. "I'd love to, and we can discuss this idea I have."

Lacey would have preferred it if Jeff had stayed up in his room, but with the aid of his crutches, he found his way down to the kitchen. That wasn't so bad, until the kids stole Hank away to show him something and they were left alone.

She tried to stay busy putting together sandwiches from the cold cuts she had in the refrigerator. When she brought plates to the table, Jeff reached for her hand and she couldn't move.

The sudden strength and heat of his touch startled her. She finally looked into his eyes. "What?"

"I'm sorry," he said. "I was out of line last night. I had no right to treat you like I did."

She took a ragged breath. She hadn't expected this, or the feelings that still lingered between them. "I have to take some of the blame. I should have left sooner."

He shook his head. "I took advantage of you, your vulnerability. It hasn't been that long since Trevor died."

She nodded, but inside she knew she hadn't been thinking about her husband when she'd been in Jeff's arms. "Sometimes it feels like he's been gone a lifetime." She nodded toward the door. "Then other times, I expect him to walk in the door any minute."

With a nod, Jeff released her hand. "The last thing I want to do is tarnish his memory." His gaze bored into hers. "We're partners now. I don't want to mess that up. So you don't have to worry about me…overstepping again."

Well, wasn't that just like a man, making all the decisions, as if *her* feelings didn't count. She leaned toward him. "In case you haven't noticed, Jeff Gentry, I'm all grown up. I can make my own decisions whether I leave or I stay. Most of all, I don't need to be protected from things. That was something Trevor never realized, and now, I'm getting the same from you. I also make my own choices." She turned and went to the refrigerator.

Jeff was at a loss, but before he found his voice, Hank returned with the kids. His granddad was smiling as Emily tugged him into the room, but not before he caught Jeff looking at Lacey and sent him a wink.

Well, darn. How had his life gotten so complicated?

"Mom, did you know that Mr. Hank doesn't have any little granddaughters my age?"

"No, I didn't." She looked at Hank. "I hear you've got a great-grandson. Zach, isn't it?"

Hank nodded. "A nice boy. But my other grandchildren seem to be taking a long time to settle down and get married."

Jeff wasn't going to get involved in this conversation.

Emily climbed into the chair beside Hank. "How many grandkids do you have?"

"Sixteen at last count, but I got a suspicion there's more coming soon."

Those big blue eyes lit up. "That's a lot. My grandpa only has two, and he lives far, far away in Flora."

"Florida," Lacey corrected.

"Florida," Emily repeated. "Maybe you need a little girl for your family."

"That's not a bad idea." Hank glanced at Lacey. "Would you and the kids be available around Labor Day? I'm in need of a cook for our cattle drive."

Jeff bit back a groan, seeing the surprised look on Lacey's face.

"Granddad, Lacey can't want—"

"Excuse me," Lacey interrupted as she came to the table. "I can answer for myself." She sent him a warning look before turning to Hank. "Exactly what would this job entail?"

"Well, I've found a replica of a chuck wagon, but I decided it would be easier to switch to a truck and refrigerated trailer." He held up a hand. "This is one of the areas we're going to update with propane stoves and grills along with a motorized vehicle. I've also been informed that the addition of portable toilets along the trail would be appreciated by the women."

"How many other women are going along?"

"There's Jeff's sister, Kelly, and you." He smiled down at Emily. "This sweet one. And I'm hoping to get Nora to ride along in the wagon. It would be nice to have a nurse along to patch up any minor scratches and cuts. There will also be a generator to keep the food cold and plenty of fresh water. And the trail isn't so far out in the wilderness that we can't get to you within thirty minutes."

Hank announced the pay for the job, and her eyes widened.

Jeff sat up straight. "I didn't know we were getting paid for this."

Hank shot him a smile. "You're family, so you already get your share from the corporation. That's the reason I came up with this, to promote more family income." He turned back to Lacey. "What do you say, Lacey? Are you interested?"

"I'll have horses to care for."

"If that's your only concern, I'll have a couple of the ranch hands take care of them for the duration," Hank countered.

Jeff watched as the kids got into the act. "Please, Mom, I want to go," Colin said. "Can I ride with the herd?"

Emily joined in, too. "Mom, I want to ride with you in the wagon. Please, say we can we go."

Lacey looked at Jeff. "I don't think the question is whether I go. Hank needs a trail boss. And he hasn't got an answer from you yet."

All eyes turned to him. Great. If he didn't know better, he'd swear this was a set-up.

Emily climbed down from her chair and came to him. "You got to go, Jeff. It's no fun without you." She climbed up onto his lap and sat there as if she belonged. "Your owie will be better, too."

"Yeah, my owie is much better. And I've already told Hank that I'll go."

He was rewarded with a big smile from the little girl. He felt his heart swell, realizing what he'd missed being away. His friend had had the life he could only dream about. He stole a glance at Lacey, knowing he couldn't have what was never his.

By week's end, things had gotten back to normal—if normal was avoiding each other. Jeff had gotten what he wanted and had moved back into the cabin. To be left alone. Funny thing was he missed the kids, but most of all, he missed Lacey.

Today though, they were together and on their way to Chance's place to check on Rebel. The stallion had performed his task, but they were waiting to see if the mares were pregnant before the horse made the trip back home.

The kids climbed out of the back of his truck. They stayed with their mother, waiting for him. Jeff tried not to think about the idea of them as a family, but it was hard not to.

"Come on, Chance said he'd be in the corral."

They all walked off toward the covered area. Although the late-afternoon Texas heat was stifling, once inside the temperature was much cooler. They went to the railing and saw two horses being ridden around the large arena.

You couldn't help but be impressed by the beautiful quarter horses. A glistening black stallion pranced as if he already knew how special he was. The other was a smaller roan filly.

"Look, Mommy," Emily said, pointing to the horses. "She's so pretty."

"Yes, she is," Lacey answered.

Jeff didn't miss the longing in her voice.

"Can I have a horse like her when I get older?" the little girl asked.

"I can't promise you that, Emily."

"I bet you could train her, Mom." Colin jumped into the conversation.

"I bet you could, too."

They all turned to find Chance Randell behind them.

He shook Jeff's hand. "Hello, kids. So you like my new additions?"

"They're pretty," Emily said.

"They're much more than that." He nodded. "The stallion is Ace in the Hole. He's a descendant of my first quarter horse, Ace High. He was the reason I wanted this place, to build my dream of breeding quarter horses."

"Looks like you got it," Lacey said.

Chance grinned. "I got so much more. This place came with bonuses—my wife, Joy, and a baby girl, Katie Rose."

Jeff glanced at Lacey. She didn't have any idea how much he longed for the same kind of life. Her gaze caught his and he looked away. "Is Ace in the Hole for sale?"

Chance seemed to be caught off guard. He pushed his hat back and studied Jeff. "That all depends. What would your plans be for him?"

"I need a good saddle horse. Also another stallion in the barn wouldn't hurt." He looked at Lacey. "What do you think, Lace? Would Ace make a good addition?"

Lacey studied the handsome horse, trying not to act surprised that Jeff asked for her opinion. "Any horse bred by Chance Randell doesn't need my approval."

Jeff grinned. "So, Uncle, are you willing to part with him?"

Chance pushed back his hat. "I don't know if I should. That would be feeding the competition." He tried to hide his smile. "But I guess we can make some sort of deal."

"And maybe a family discount?" Jeff asked.

His uncle slapped him on his back. "You are definitely a Randell." They both laughed.

Lacey liked seeing this side of Jeff. It reminded her of their youth and those carefree days.

Planting the kids on the railing, Chance escorted Lacey and Jeff inside the arena. While Chance and Jeff went to see Ace, Lacey kept her attention on the filly.

"She's a beauty, isn't she? And a fast learner." The young rider climbed down and raised his fingers to his hat in greeting. "Hello, I'm Will Hansen. My dad is Chance's breeder and trainer."

"Lacey Guthrie." She patted the horse's neck and the animal bobbed its head, enjoying the attention. "What's her name?"

"Summer Mist. We call her Misty."

The filly nudged her when she stopped the stroking. "So you like that, do you, girl?"

The two men joined them. "Looks like someone else has found a horse," Jeff said.

She froze. "Oh, no. She's just so sweet. Besides, we can't afford another horse."

Chance smiled. "Since she's my youngest daughter's horse, Misty's not for sale anyway. Ellie's away in England on a student-exchange program. But I wanted you to see her, and ask if you'd be willing to work with her."

Lacey was taken aback. "But you train your own horses."

"Saddle and cutters, mostly." Chance rubbed the horse's muzzle. "She's special. Ellie wants Misty to compete in reining." He turned back to Lacey. "And I think you'd be the best person for the job."

Jeff came up behind her, placing his arm across her shoulders as if he did it all the time. "Looks like you've started your training business."

CHAPTER TEN

AN hour later, they'd set a fair price for the horse's training and made arrangements for Misty to be moved to the Guthrie Ranch. Jeff gathered the kids to the truck and asked if they wanted to go out to supper in town. Hearing the cheers, he smiled and they headed for a popular pizza place at the edge of town.

After everyone had ordered their favorite food, Jeff handed out coins to Emily and Colin with instructions that the older brother watch his little sister. Reluctantly, Colin guided Emily to the rows of video games while Jeff carried two iced teas to the booth in the corner.

This wouldn't be the place he'd choose to take Lacey, but he liked them all being together. Not that this was a date, but he'd take any time he could get with her. It had been a long week without her and the kids. Yeah, he'd definitely missed Emily and Colin, too.

Since he'd insisted on leaving their house, he'd spent lonely evenings up at the cabin, with Chance checking on him now and then. He'd only seen Lacey when he'd gone to the ranch to work. At the end of the day, she hadn't even invited him to stay for supper. Not that he blamed her for holding back on the invitations, not after the way he'd acted as her houseguest. His idea of keeping his distance had well and truly backfired on him.

He placed the drinks on the table and sat down. "While the kids are busy at the machines, I want to talk to you."

She looked at him with those big green eyes, causing him to lose his train of thought.

"Things moved pretty fast today at Chance's place and I want to make sure you're okay with training Misty."

She leaned back. "It's going to be tight, and it will take time away from Fancy, but I'd like to go for it."

"I'll help as much as I can," he told her, hoping she wouldn't rebuff him. "Maybe it's time you quit your job at the market."

Her expression changed so quickly he had to clarify his reasons. "Before you start to argue, I've checked into group insurance packages, and with the extra money from the horses we're boarding, and now your training, we can afford it. I have the feeling that once people know you're working with one of Chance's horses, other owners will take notice of your talents." He glanced away. "I also talked with Will Hansen about working part-time for us. That will free up more time for you. He can also do the exercising and grooming."

Lacey was silent for a long time. "What about health insurance for the kids?"

"It's affordable since we've formed a partnership and it's all in the package I mentioned."

Lacey was silent for a long time, then said, "Seems like you've been making a lot of plans. I wish you had come to me about hiring Will."

"I didn't hire him, yet. I told him I had to check with my partner first."

She nodded. "I appreciate that. One of the big problems Trevor and I had was when he tried to handle everything on his own. We all know how that worked out." She looked so sad. "All I ask from you, Jeff, is that I get a say in making the decisions."

He never wanted to cause her pain again. "I promise, Lace. I want this to work between us."

Jeff pulled his truck up to the cabin. He shut off the engine and the outdoors suddenly went dark, but he waited for his eyes to adjust to the moonlight shining over the shack.

Home sweet home.

He definitely needed a generator. No, what he really needed was his own place. Even though he officially owned this land, he'd always intended to give it back to Lacey. That hadn't stopped him from thinking about building a bigger place, a house on the prime piece of land. It would be across the creek, on the rise overlooking the area.

Of course, his granddad Hank owned one of the sweetest spots, Mustang Valley. A home to protect his wild ponies. It was also the site of Randell Nature Retreat for guests who wanted to enjoy the peace and quiet. Jeff glanced around. Even in the dark, he knew this place could attract people, too. He just wasn't sure he wanted to share it with strangers.

He made his way to the porch, but didn't go inside. The night heat kept him from being in a hurry. Though he valued his solitude, he found he missed the kids' noisy chatter.

He mostly missed Lacey. The way she looked, the way she smelled, especially that fresh citrus fragrance of her hair. Even after she worked with the horses, it still lingered on her. His body stirred, and he didn't like it. His entire adult life he'd been disciplined, except when it came to Lacey.

He heard a noise and tensed. It came from the side of the cabin where he kept the trash bin. He unlocked the door, grabbing a flashlight off the counter and the handgun from the shelf. He wasn't sure what he'd encounter.

Hesitantly, he stepped off the porch and rounded the corner. His flashlight illuminated the area next to the cans. That was where he found the mangiest dog he'd ever seen. His brown and sable fur was matted and dirty, and worse, he was all skin and bones. The animal gave him a soulful look as he wagged his tail.

"Aren't you a sad-looking thing?" He slipped the sidearm in the waistband of his jeans, knelt down and held out his hand. Country roads were a dumping ground for unwanted pets.

With its ears pinned back, the mutt took a tentative step and sniffed his hand. "You could use a good meal."

Jeff went inside the cabin, lit the lanterns so he could see what he was doing, then began rummaging around the cupboard to see what he had to feed the animal. Way in the back of the top shelf he found a can of stew. He pulled it out and something fell down. Looking closer, he discovered it was some kind of book or ledger. He set it on the counter, then opened the can for his intruder. After he dumped the stew into a bowl, he set it on the porch, along with a towel for the dog to sleep on. If he was still there in the morning, then he'd decide what to do. Until then the animal wasn't coming inside. He closed the door and looked at the lone bunk.

Solitude. Wasn't that what he'd wanted since coming home? Sure. He should be used to being alone.

He sat down at the table and rubbed a hand over his face. Tonight he was restless. His thoughts turned to his friend and Jeff got a sudden ache in his chest, making it hard for him to breathe. He missed Trevor, missed the years they could have had together if he hadn't been so hung up on Lacey. Yet how could he have come back when he coveted someone else's wife?

He went to turn off the lantern when he saw the notebook on the counter. It was probably left over from the years the Guthries ran cattle through here and kept track.

He opened it and discovered it wasn't that at all. It was a journal, written by Trevor.

Jeff sank back into the chair, adjusted the lantern and turned to the first page. It was dated nearly ten years ago. He read through a few of the early entries. Trevor's wedding. The day Jeff left for the army. The births of his children. His breath caught as he flipped to the last page and found a letter addressed to him, dated August tenth—nearly a year ago.

Jeff,

So you found my journal. Why am I not surprised you came back to the cabin? It's been a long time, friend. Even though I should be angry that you haven't been around much, I missed those times when we could just escape up here.

The hours we sat by the creek and talked about life.

Oh, it was so simple back then. Our biggest problem was how to stay out of trouble in class or with our parents. Boy, we learned a lot together, but a lot we had to find out on our own. I miss you, friend.

Another entry a week later.

Jeff,

Today is a bad time for me. I received some news from my doctor. It wasn't good. I didn't handle it well, so I had Lacey drive me up here for a few hours. She always understands when I need time by myself. It's funny how this place always gave me that peace. Most of all, I feel close to you here. You have no idea how badly I want you to come through that door.

Three days later.

Jeff,

This morning, I was told that I'm dying. Funny, isn't it? I'm barely thirty, I catch a cold and a virus damages my heart. There's nothing they can do but put me on a donor list, and they're not optimistic that I have the time to wait for a new heart.

So I came up here and cried like a baby.

I need you, friend. I wish I had your strength to help me through this. I know you can't drop everything just to be with me and I have to deal with that. Even worse, I also have to deal with the fact that I'll be leaving Lacey and the kids alone. They're my life.

Jeff had to put the book down at that moment. He didn't think he could read any more about the life he'd envied for so long. What kind of friend did that make him?

The next morning, Jeff pulled up next to the barn two hours late. Since Will had started work today, he wasn't worried that Lacey was left to do it all.

He wouldn't be worth much today, anyway, since he hadn't slept last night. He'd ended up sitting on the porch, thinking about Trevor, trying to put the past to rest, letting a silly mutt keep him company. There were still so many unanswered questions. He didn't understand everything that Trevor had been trying to say.

Did he know of his betrayal with Lacey? They were so young and stupid back then. And in the end Lacey had chosen Trevor over him. She'd married him.

Jeff stepped down from the truck and looked back inside to see the dog, hesitating to get out. He knew the feeling.

After the dog had been checked out at the vet and had an extra-long bath and flea dip, the border-collie mix didn't look too bad. And he had a home now.

"Come on, boy. There are a couple of kids that'll be crazy about you." He reached for the leash and helped the too-thin animal down to the ground.

He walked into the corral and saw Lacey working Fancy. This had become one of the highlights of his day, watching her with the filly. His thoughts also flashed to

Trevor's journal. He'd kept calling Jeff *friend.* How could that be? Jeff had broken the code of honor when he'd made love to Lacey. Even if it were ten years ago, he knew the feelings for her were still there. For him anyway.

Lacey looked in his direction, then rode over to the railing.

"Who's your friend?"

He tipped his hat back. "Not sure, he paid a visit to the cabin last night." He glanced down at the dog sitting next to him. "I took him to my cousin Lindsey's veterinary office to have him checked out. Then we went to the groomer's."

Lacey climbed down from the horse and tied the reins to the railing. She examined the dog closely. "He's one pathetic-looking animal."

Jeff didn't think he looked so bad. "You should have seen him earlier. His coat was so matted they had to trim it short. He's also missed a few meals."

Lacey knelt down and held out her hand. The dog took a tentative step closer, sniffed and then licked it. "What's his name?"

Jeff shrugged. "Don't know. Should I ask him?"

"Very funny, Gentry. You have to call him something."

"I'm not even sure I'll keep him."

She frowned. "You can't take him to the pound."

"Oh, a doggie," Emily cried and came running.

Jeff held up a hand. "Easy, Emily, I'm not sure how he'll act around kids."

The child ignored him and began petting the dog. The mutt just looked up at the girl with those big soulful eyes. It was instant love.

Jeff glanced at the smile on Lacey's face. He knew the feeling.

Colin joined them. "Hey, whose dog? Man, he sure is ugly."

"He's Jeff's," Emily said. "And he's not ugly. He's just sad. I wish we could have a dog."

Jeff looked at Lacey.

"Oh, no, your friend is not staying here," she said. "I have enough to take care of."

"But, Mom, we'll take care of him," Emily said. "He can sleep in my room."

Colin spoke up. "Oh, no. He'll get lost in all your stuffed animals. And you'll dress him up."

As if the animal understood, he shot a look at Colin. "He can stay in my room," the boy said.

Jeff caught another warning look from Lacey. "How about he stays with me for now? It gets lonely up at the cabin."

"You can move back to our house," Emily suggested.

He didn't miss Lacey's uneasiness. "I think old Lonesome here and I need to stay at the cabin for now."

"I like that name," Colin said. "Can we play with Lonesome now?"

"If it's okay with your mother."

She nodded.

They cheered and took the leather leash from Jeff. "I have food and water dishes in the truck," he called to them. "Keep him out on the porch, I'm not sure he's housebroken."

The happy kids took off with the suddenly perky dog.

"You are such a phony," Lacey began. "Mr. Tough, ex-military guy, takes in strays."

He liked her teasing. His pulse began to race as his gaze moved to her lips. That wasn't all he enjoyed about her. "It takes one to know one, Lace. You took *me* in."

She didn't seem to have a comeback for that. "I'd better get back to work."

He nodded and followed her to the barn. He was wanting like hell to fit in here again. He wanted a home. But so much depended on Lacey. He knew the one thing he didn't want was to be just one of her strays.

Two weeks passed before Jeff and Lacey were able to get out to Brandon and Nora's place. The ranch had once been his cousin's maternal grandfather's spread with a small section that bordered Mustang Valley. Brandon had inherited it along with his two siblings, and they'd ended up dividing the land and the cattle operation between the three of them. Brandon had chosen law enforcement as a career, but had moved his new wife and her son, Zach, to the ranch about a year ago.

Jeff pulled up just as Nora and Brandon came out of the two-story yellow-and-white house to greet them.

He was used to the impressive Randell Ranch, but Lacey was busy taking in the numerous outbuildings and the pristine white fencing, not to mention the large house.

"This is unbelievable," Lacey said.

"Someday the Guthrie Ranch will look like this." He climbed out of the truck and came around to her side as Brandon came up to them.

They shook hands. "You made it."

Nora welcomed Lacey with a hug. "I'm so glad we

finally got together." She turned to the kids. "These must be your children."

Emily stepped forward with a smile. "I'm Emily, and this is my brother, Colin. I'm five and he's eight, but he'll be nine on his birthday in two weeks."

Nora leaned down. "Well, I'm Nora and I'm happy to meet you both," she told them. "My son, Zach, is helping to get the horses saddled. We thought we'd ride out to Mustang Valley today and have a picnic."

"Cool!" Colin cheered. "Will we see wild mustangs?"

"If we're lucky."

They all headed toward the corral where there were six mounts ready for the ride. Although Zach was the same age as Colin, he wasn't as tall. The dark-haired boy was friendly, and finally Lacey's son began to open up.

"Okay, let's head out," Brandon said.

Zach showed Colin to his horse, Bandit, and Emily to the small mare named Sugar. A strange feeling took over as Jeff helped adjust the stirrups for Emily. This was a family outing. Over the past month, he'd gotten close to these kids. He glanced at Lacey. Their mother was a different story. Since that night in the bedroom, she had kept her distance.

Jeff glanced at Brandon to see him pull his wife close and kiss her. "Nora's going to drive out and meet us there," he told everyone as he touched her slightly rounded stomach. "She's expecting a baby and we're not taking any chances with our little one."

Brandon mounted his gelding, then they all tossed a wave to Nora and headed out of the corral toward the trail. Jeff rode up beside Lacey. "I haven't ridden out here since I was a kid." He sat up in the saddle, feeling good about how easily he handled the horse. "Trevor and I came out here once and we camped out with Brandon and his dad. We should have invited you along."

Lacey smiled. "I hadn't moved to San Angelo by then. Besides, were girls even invited?"

Jeff stole a look at the beautiful woman riding beside him. "At ten years old, we weren't into girls yet." Not until the day Lacey Haynes walked into their seventh-grade class. "We might have made an exception for you, though."

Lacey tugged on her horse's reins as they rode to the ridge and looked down at the rich, grassy valley where several trees lined the rocky-bottom creek. Ancient oaks dotted the slopes, nearly hiding the nature cabins from view.

Jeff stopped beside her. "It's still as pretty as I remember." He leaned on the saddle horn and took it all in. "Over the years, Hank added the cabins when they started up the nature retreat. To preserve the area, and protect the mustangs, there aren't any vehicles allowed in the area. They use golf carts to bring in guests, or they ride in on horseback."

"This is incredible." She looked at him. "I thought the area around our cabin was pretty, but this—"

"Hey, I love that old cabin."

Brandon rode up. "How do you like it so far?"

"It's beautiful," Lacey said.

Brandon sighed. "Yeah, I never get tired of the view."

"I want to see the mustangs," Emily said.

"We will," Brandon promised. "First, we eat lunch. If we're quiet the mustangs will show up. Well, we'd better get moving. Nora's waiting at the cabin over on the ridge."

"Then let's go," Jeff said. "I'm suddenly hungry."

They took off across the valley to the cabin where Nora had tables set up on the porch. A tray of sandwiches and salads were waiting. After washing the dirt off, they sat down on the cabin porch and enjoyed the family meal. The kids were chatting away. The boys even included Emily, who seemed to be mesmerized by Zach.

"Look, the mustangs," the girl cried and turned to her mom. "Can we go see them?"

"I don't know, honey, we might scare them off."

Brandon stood. "I think we could get a little closer if we're quiet."

The kids followed Brandon and Nora as they walked down toward the creek. Jeff watched Lacey begin to pick up the lunch mess, but he stopped her.

"We'll do this later, you're coming with me."

She tried to argue, but he grabbed her hand and walked her down the slope. Once they reached the grove of trees, they paused as a mare and her filly wandered into view. Emily was trying hard to keep quiet but she was dancing around with excitement.

"Oh, Jeff. Look at them." Lacey glanced over her shoulder to him. "I wish I had a camera."

He moved in close, inhaling her fresh scent. "I guess I'll just have to bring you back here."

She turned again. "I'll hold you to that." She studied him with those sweet green eyes. "I bet you brought a lot of girls here."

He shook his head. "I never did." He only wanted

to share this with Lacey. "I would have brought you, but I doubted you'd have come."

She turned around. They were standing close, her back against a tree. Normally, he'd take advantage of the situation, but the kids were too close.

"You never asked me," she said.

His heart skipped and began to pound in double time. "I'm asking you now."

CHAPTER ELEVEN

LATER that night, back at his cabin, Jeff sat outside on the porch, Lonesome lying at his feet. The dog hadn't left his side since he'd returned home.

Jeff knew the feeling. After spending the day with Lacey, he hadn't wanted to leave her, either. How could he have said those things to her? He recalled Trevor's words from his journal. *Lacey's my life.*

Maybe coming back home was a mistake. The wanting hadn't stopped. All the longing for her over the past years had never gone away. Yet actually having Lacey as his seemed like a dream—albeit an impossible one. He couldn't exactly ask Trevor's permission.

The sound of an engine interrupted his solitude. He stood as Lacey's truck pulled up. Panic hit him as he stood and she got out. Was something wrong?

She walked up to the porch. All he saw was her silhouette in the shadows. "Lacey, what's wrong? Is it the kids?" He knew they had stayed for a sleepover at Brandon and Nora's house.

She shook her head. "I wanted to see you."

His heart didn't slow as she stepped closer. "See me about what?"

"Can't I just want to be here?"

"Sure. I can understand you're lonely without the kids—"

"Did you mean what you said today?" she interrupted. "Did you want to ask me out?"

Suddenly he felt as if everything was going too fast, but he couldn't lie to her. "Yes."

She didn't hesitate and wrapped her arms around him.

Oh, God, he couldn't deal with this. "Lacey, maybe we should talk about this…tomorrow." It killed him, but he slipped from her embrace.

She looked up. "You want me to go?"

He was trembling, he wanted her so badly. "It might be better if you did." He thought about what had happened all those years ago, and how guilty he'd felt.

Inside he was praying she wouldn't leave. He couldn't resist, and pressed a kiss against her forehead, then her eyelids, moving downward to the corner of her tempting mouth. "Lace, we can't start this…"

"Why, Jeff? We already know it'll be good between us."

"It would be too good," he breathed. "I'm not the man for you, I'm still trying to figure things out. To accept who I am."

"I've accepted you, Jeff." Her hand covered his. "But it seems like you're not ready to accept me, or the possibility of us."

It seemed impossible even to think they could finally be together. He'd waited so long.

She pulled away. "Thank you for the perfect day, Jeff. I'll leave."

He held on to her. "Don't go, Lace." He drew her close. "But you'd better be sure."

"I don't want to think about the past or the future right now. I just want this moment with you." Her voice lowered. "Make love to me, Jeff."

He lost it. He leaned down and captured her mouth, ending her words. He only wanted to hear her sounds of pleasure. If nothing else, he was going to make sure she felt that tonight.

He broke off the kiss and swung her up into his arms. Inside, with only one lantern lit, the cabin was dim. It was also warm, but he wanted to make love to her in a bed. Even if it was just a bunk.

He put her down next to the single bed, happy he'd removed the top bunk. "God, Lace, I've thought about this since I left your house. When you came into my room."

She touched his face. "This time, I'm not leaving, Jeff. I want to share everything with you tonight." She tugged his T-shirt over his head, then went for the drawstring on his sweats.

Stopping her, he forced a smile. "Ladies first." When he had undressed her, she stood, allowing him to take her all in.

"Now, it's your turn," she insisted.

He released a breath, and sat down on the bed, then reached under the leg of his sweatpants. He removed his prosthesis and set it aside. His heart was pounding, his fears were about to overpower him, but he kept his focus on her eyes.

"The other night, I didn't want you to stop," she admitted. "I definitely don't want to stop now."

Jeff closed his eyes as she kissed him. He didn't want to bring up the past. There was no guilt here. This time it was only about them. "I don't want to stop either." He just wasn't sure if he could pull it off. He hadn't made love in a long time, not since before he'd been wounded.

Her questioning gaze locked with his. Then her hands went to his sweatpants and slowly began tugging them down his body, until finally they were off. She tossed the clothes on the floor, but her gaze never left his body.

"You are one beautiful man, Jeff Gentry. You always were."

He was glad the light in the cabin was dim. He didn't like being on display, even before he'd lost his leg. Yet, he didn't want to shy away from Lacey. "You're the one who's beautiful."

She kissed him again. Her fingers traced over his skin. "I have a lot of scars, too, Jeff. I've had babies."

"I don't see anything but perfection," he told her honestly.

Her gaze moved over him as her hand brushed down his leg. He tensed, holding his breath as she stroked his knee, then further down to where his leg used to be. "From what I can see, you're pretty much perfect, too." Her gaze returned to his face. "Except maybe your ears stick out a little." She leaned over and kissed him on his surprised mouth.

He quickly flipped her on her back. "Maybe we can find something we're perfect at together." He took her mouth in a hungry kiss. One night with her wouldn't satisfy him. He needed a lifetime with this woman, and he knew that wouldn't even be enough.

The next morning wasn't awkward at all because Jeff didn't stay in the bed. It had been years since he'd analyzed his feelings for Lacey. He didn't want to find regret in her eyes, so he decided to get up and give her time to herself.

After pulling on his prosthesis and sweatpants, he'd started for the door when he saw the journal on the counter. Damn that book. Damn Trevor for even writing anything to him.

He went outside, where he and Lonesome made their way down to the creek. But all he could think about was the woman he'd left in his bed. The woman he loved. But would she ever be his? His biggest fear was that she would always belong to his best friend.

Regret and sadness rushed over Lacey as Jeff walked out of the cabin, the click of the door latch seeming to signal the finality on her previous life with Trevor. She hadn't given one thought to her husband during the night. It had been the first time in years she'd been able to think about Jeff without guilt.

It had been Jeff who'd brought her pleasure such as she'd never known. It had been Jeff who'd worshiped her body with his touch, praised her with hushed promises of passion.

Lacey brushed away a tear, recalling all those years ago. Had Jeff loved her back then? If she had asked him, would he have stayed and accepted his responsibility for their afternoon of passion? She'd never know. He'd left without a second glance. He'd left not knowing she'd gotten pregnant with his child. A baby she'd lost before she'd gotten the chance to hold, to nurture it. She'd lost them both. If it hadn't been for Trevor...

She wiped away another tear. No, she wouldn't let

Jeff hurt her again. She wouldn't make any more mistakes. She had her children to think about.

Lacey sat up, reached for her clothes and began to dress. Once her boots were on, she combed her fingers through her hair as she headed for the door, and with as much dignity as she could manage, she walked out.

Outside, the sun made her squint as she looked around. Even if he wanted to be alone, she couldn't just leave without saying anything. She wasn't that much of a coward. She walked toward the creek, where she spotted Jeff sitting under the trees on a rock.

He hadn't put on a shirt, given his quick departure, and he looked sexy. She hated that she still wanted this man. But she was grown now and didn't expect any confessions of love.

The dog caught sight of her and came running. She knelt down to pet the animal as Jeff stood and then walked up the hill.

They stared at each other, and then she finally spoke. "Morning."

"Good morning." He glanced around as if he were nervous. "I can fix us some breakfast if you're hungry."

Lacey didn't want food. She wanted the same thing she'd wanted ten years ago. For him to take her into his arms and tell her that he wanted her again and wanted to make things work out between them. But he didn't and she had to face that fact.

"This is strange for me, Gentry. I've never done the morning-after regret thing." She drew a breath and rushed on. "No, that's wrong. Didn't we have this same awkward moment about ten years ago? Only that time you walked out on me."

He looked miserable as he came closer. "Lacey, I

couldn't regret anything if I tried, not then or now." He hesitated then, and confessed, "I don't know where to go from here, Lace."

"We don't have to go anywhere, Jeff." She took his hand. "If you're worried I expect something because we had sex last night—don't."

"That's not what I meant. I'm not sure if you're ready for this. Trevor's only been gone a few months."

"It's ten months, and don't bring Trevor into this."

"How can I not? You were married to him. He was my best friend."

"Yes, he was my husband," she said. "But I didn't betray him, Jeff. Not last night, or ten years ago when we made love. So don't try and make me feel guilty."

She could see that she wasn't getting through to him. She was crazy to think they'd renewed their past feelings. It was evident who he was loyal to. Had she just been the pawn between the two men?

She turned to leave, but he reached for her. "Please, Lacey, I need to make you understand. I want things to be different."

She fought with as much pride as she could hold on to and broke his hold on her arm. "Oh, I understand all right. We need to forget last night ever happened, just like the last time."

He started to speak, but didn't.

And that was all Lacey had to say. She turned and marched to the truck. Trouble was, how did she erase the fact that she'd fallen in love with Jeff Gentry all over again?

By afternoon, Jeff was on his fourth beer. He usually didn't drink, mainly because he didn't like not being in control. And because his biological father had been a drunk and got abusive. But at this moment, he didn't care about any of that.

As he popped another tab and took a long drink, he placed his feet up along the porch railing. Lonesome, lying in the spot next to his chair, suddenly took off barking. Jeff looked toward the pasture and blinked. Cows. The sound of mooing filled his aching head.

"What on earth?" He stood and walked around the cabin. Off in the distance there were about two dozen head of Herefords coming his way. Behind the herd were two riders, Brandon, of course, and his brother, Jay.

The cows were directed to the larger grassy pasture, and when his cousins rode his way, Jeff noticed Brandon was leading another saddled mount. "Oh, no, not today," he groaned.

"Hey, cuz," Brandon called with a big grin. "You ready to go to work?"

"You ever thought about giving a guy some warning?"

Brandon leaned against the saddle horn. "So you can ditch me? No way, cowboy." He turned to his brother. "You can head back, Jay. I have this under control."

Jay grinned. "Have fun."

Jeff watched the younger Randell take off and Brandon climbed off his horse as the cattle settled down to graze in the high grass. He came toward Jeff, pulling off his gloves. "So, you going to offer me a drink and tell me about it?"

Great. "Tell you about what?"

Brandon frowned. "Lacey shows up to pick up the

kids looking like she's lost her best friend, then says she's taking them to see Trevor's parents in Florida."

"What?" He couldn't let her go. "When is she leaving?"

"She's already left." Brandon frowned. "She didn't tell you?"

Jeff shook his head. He didn't deserve to know anything about her. "No."

"You'd think partners would tell each other these things." Brandon walked the horses toward the lean-to and tied their reins to the post. "What happened yesterday, Jeff? Everything seemed great between you two. Did you fight?"

They walked around to the front of the cabin. Brandon started to go inside, then stopped. "This place is like an oven." Grabbing a couple of waters, they headed toward the shade of the creek with two fold-up lawn chairs.

"Okay, you dropped Lacey off last night and everything was okay between you two."

"Later, she came out to the cabin."

Brandon's mouth broke into a grin, then faded. "You didn't send her home, did you?"

Jeff glanced away. "I should have."

"Well, finally," Brandon said, his smile returning. "I take it you two...got together?"

Jeff leaned forward, his elbows on his knees. "I told her that maybe it was a mistake, it might be too soon for her."

Brandon groaned. "You actually got a chance with her, and you tell her that?" His cousin sprang to his feet. "I was wrong. No man would ever turn away a woman like Lacey."

"I'm not like you. I'm not a Randell."

"The hell you aren't. You're as much a part of this family as I am. Damn it, man, you've proved that by screwing up so royally. Most men in this family love their women forever. That could be because Jack was such a womanizer." He stared at Jeff. "So how long have you loved Lacey?"

Jeff shrugged, mumbling, "Since seventh grade."

Brandon shook his head. "Did she even have breasts then?"

All at once Jeff threw back his head and laughed. "Who can remember?"

"Well, remember this, she came to you last night. So that means she has feelings for you."

"You don't understand, Lacey and I have history." He looked at Brandon. "Before I went into the army, I came up here to talk to her, to say goodbye. We made love."

Brandon whistled softly. "What about Trevor?"

"No, she and Trevor had broken up that summer. The problem was he'd been the one who begged me to talk to her, to help them get back together."

Brandon leaned forward. "Instead, you broke the guy code and slept with your friend's girl."

Jeff nodded.

"Come on, Jeff. It might have been a lousy thing to do ten years ago, but everything worked out. Trevor got the girl, and you went into the military. Now, it's your chance, fair and square. I'd say that Lacey coming here last night was a pretty good indication she wants to be with you."

"What if it's just because she's lonely, and I'm convenient?"

"This isn't about your leg, is it? Oh, I know what it is." He snapped his fingers. "She cringed during sex because of your leg."

Jeff could still feel Lacey's hands on his injured leg, touching him where he was the most vulnerable. Her trust and caring had just enhanced their lovemaking.

"No, I just don't know if I'm the man she needs in her life." And there were the kids. Not that he didn't love them already, but could he be the dad they needed?

"You think because you're missing part of your leg you can't have a life? Can't have the woman you love? A family?" Brandon didn't wait for an answer. "So I should tell my son, Zach, that because he's diabetic he can't go after what he wants?"

"Of course not," Jeff argued, hating that his cousin knew him so well.

"Good, because I'm never going to let Zach give up on anything. Unlike you, who won't fight for what you want. Come on, man, you have a second chance, don't use being an amputee as an excuse." Brandon stood and started toward the cabin. "We better get to work and herd some cattle before the drive. Unless you think you can't handle it."

Jeff wasn't looking forward to sitting on a horse most of the day, but he needed to build up his leg strength, and get used to long hours in the saddle.

He grabbed two more bottles of water from the cooler and they headed to the horses. "Okay, what if I go after Lacey and it doesn't work out?"

Brandon climbed on his gelding. "There are no guarantees with love, but you can't win, Jeff, if you don't try. I can't tell you how many times, even when Nora pushed me away, that I kept going back. I couldn't give up. I loved her too much. For heaven's sake, Jeff, Lacey came here last night. That means she's decided she wants to give a relationship with you a try."

Jeff's spirits soared with hope, but just as quickly sank. He needed to talk to Lacey. He swung his leg over his horse. "I know I'll probably be sorry I asked, but do you have any suggestions on how to win her back?"

Lacey was happy to be home. It had been a long, miserable week, and she'd missed Jeff more than she wanted to admit. Even though Trevor's parents had showed them a good time, the kids had missed home, too. They wouldn't stop talking about Jeff. Even the Guthries figured out that he had become a big part of their lives. They'd always liked Trevor's friend, and in so many words gave Lacey their blessing to move on with her life. Would they feel that way if they knew the truth about what had happened ten years ago between them?

After a week, Lacey knew she had to return to Texas. Even though Jeff didn't want her, she had a ranch and a business to run. She had to face her partner sometime.

That was the problem. Over and over she'd relived her night with Jeff. And now, somehow, she had to put that out of her mind and find a way to be able to work with him.

Since she would have to spend three days on the cattle drive with the man, she'd better figure it out fast. Luckily, they wouldn't be alone much, and she wasn't riding with the herd. She only had to get to the designated spots and serve meals for the twenty riders. She would have help, Nora and Jeff's sister, Kelly.

At 5:00 a.m. that morning, she and a pair of excited kids headed for the Circle B Ranch where the first Annual Randell Ranch Cattle Drive was set to begin.

She walked into the main dining hall, already crowded with eager guests. She and the kids got in line and filled their plates and went to sit with Nora and Zach.

"Good, you're here," Nora said. "Jeff wants to have a quick meeting before they take off."

She didn't want to talk to Jeff. "But we're just driving out to the first stop on the trail."

Nora frowned, glanced at the kids talking at the table, and then took Lacey's hand. "Come with me."

Lacey reluctantly got up and followed her new friend to the empty side of the room. "Brandon told me what happened between you and Jeff before you left town." She raised a hand. "I don't need details. I do know it's easy to do crazy things when it comes to the Randell men." There was concern on Nora's face. "Maybe if you and Jeff talk—"

"No," Lacey interrupted. "I've made a fool of myself over him more than once and Jeff's made it clear how he feels."

"Okay, but so you know, he regrets how things turned out."

Her heart raced. "So do I. I never should have gone to the cabin. I won't make that mistake again."

"You still want to go on this trip, don't you?"

"Of course, the kids are looking forward to it. And I told Hank I would go. It's too late to replace me." She blinked back tears. "And I'm not going to dump this all on you with you being pregnant."

"Lacey."

She froze on hearing Jeff call her name. She turned as he walked toward her. He was dressed in his standard Western shirt and jeans covered in a pair of black leather chaps. His hat was pulled down on his forehead, his expression serious. She could also see the other women in the room staring at him.

He managed a half smile. "I'm glad you're back. Did you have a good visit with the Guthries?"

Suddenly the room emptied. "Yes. They send their regards."

His eyes connected with hers. "Lacey, I know I'm the reason you left."

She jerked her gaze away. "Don't flatter yourself, Gentry. I had this trip planned for a while," she fibbed. Seeing his hurt, she nearly apologized but held her nerve. "Nora said you needed to talk to me about the cattle drive."

He pulled off a sheet of paper from the clipboard. "Here's the schedule and a map. I could vary it, but I'm hoping not by much." His dark gaze met hers again. "I'm sorry, Lacey. The last thing I wanted to do was hurt you."

She took a shaky breath. "I hurt myself, Jeff. But at least I was honest about my feelings. Excuse me, I need to help get Colin ready to leave."

She started off, but Jeff reached for her arm, forcing her to look at him. "If I owe you anything, Lacey, it's honesty, and I hope you're ready for it. Because when we return from this trip, we're going to deal with us."

Lacey watched him walk away. Honesty. She doubted that Jeff Gentry knew the meaning of the word—not now or ten years ago when he'd walked away from her. He'd never stayed to see if she was okay, or if she could possibly be pregnant with his child.

CHAPTER TWELVE

So far the first day of the cattle drive hadn't gone too badly.

Jeff rubbed his thigh as he sat in the saddle. He turned to watch the wranglers on horseback as they rode drag behind the herd. They'd made good time through the morning. The only mishap had been when one man went after a runaway calf. He got his horse tangled up in some mesquite. Two of the experienced ranch hands took control and got him out. Luckily, the horse only had minor scratches.

Cousin Lindsey had been waiting for them when they arrived at the chuck wagon for lunch. After cleaning the horse's wounds, she then deemed the gelding well enough to go on.

If anything could deter him from becoming a cattleman, today had been the day. Yet he did want the ranch life, and the more time he'd spent with his Uncle Chance and working with Lacey, he knew raising quarter horses was what he wanted to do. He still had a lot to learn about the breeding business. Luckily, he had a lot to draw on among the Randells, including his dad and uncle. They all ran a successful company.

That was what he wanted to make of G&G Quarter Horses—a success. Eventually he wanted to expand, even build his own place. He'd already been checking out a way to grow the business to make it as much Gentry as Guthrie.

Right now everything at the ranch had Trevor's stamp on it. Not that he wanted to take anything away from his friend, but he needed to make his own mark. That could happen soon, but he still had to talk to Jay before he could go to Lacey with the idea of leasing some pasture land, and even selling some of the ranch's spring water.

His thoughts turned to the woman who had been on his mind and in his heart forever. What if he'd already blown it, and she never forgave him? He shut his eyes, unable to stop thinking about the night she'd showed up at the cabin. Even before he'd lost his leg, he'd never been one to let anyone get too close, except Trevor and Lacey. It scared the hell out of him.

He cursed himself for his own insecurities about the past and for letting her leave that morning. If he got another chance, he definitely wouldn't do it again.

"Hey, there's no sleeping on the job," Brandon called as he rode up next to him.

They fell into an easy pace alongside the herd. "I'm the boss here," Jeff joked.

"If you say so." Smiling, his cousin glanced around. "How are you doing?"

"Not too bad, outside of the heat, and the fact I'll probably be sore later, but the leg doesn't seem to be giving me any trouble." He rubbed his thigh again. "I hate saying this, but you were right about putting in time on horseback the past two weeks."

Brandon nodded. "Good. Have you had a chance to talk to Lacey?"

He shook his head. "This isn't the best place for a serious talk."

"You can be subtle, but let her know you're not letting her get away."

"When did you turn into such a matchmaker?"

Brandon shrugged. "Nora, I guess. I never knew I could be this happy. So don't give up on Lacey."

Jeff knew how hard his cousin had worked to win Nora. She might have loved the sheriff's deputy who'd rescued her more than once, but her abusive ex-husband had made her extremely leery of trusting again.

"Catch you later," his cousin said as he kicked his horse's side and shot off, then met up with nine-year-old Zach. Watching the two together, Jeff could see they were truly father and son.

He drew a ragged breath. Could he be that for Lacey's kids? They seemed to like him enough, but how would they feel about him loving their mother? Taking their dad's place in the house? Whoa. Maybe he should get another opinion. He caught sight of Lacey's son on his horse riding with Brandon and Zach.

Jeff pressed his heels into his horse and pulled up beside the boy. "Hey, Colin, you want to ride up ahead with me? We'll scout out the trail."

"Cool," the boy said.

Yeah, Jeff thought it was cool, too. Would the boy feel that way after he pled his case?

"Brandon, could you and Zach watch things for a while?" Jeff asked.

"Sure." His cousin looked down at his son. "We can handle it, can't we, Zach?"

The boy nodded. "Sure." Brandon waved them off.

The pair picked up the pace and headed down the old service road, no longer used except to check on the cattle.

Jeff glanced overhead at the scattered clouds. "I hope it's not going to rain. We'll have a lot of wet wranglers."

Colin didn't laugh.

"Is there something wrong, son?"

The boy shrugged. "Mom's been sad. And I don't know why she suddenly made us go to Papa and Grandma Guthrie's."

Jeff shifted in the saddle. "You ever think maybe your mom was tired and needed some time away?" He'd bet he was the cause of Lacey's misery. He hated that, but it also gave him a spark of hope.

"Yeah, but she's crying again like she did after Dad died."

Okay, Jeff didn't like that.

The boy looked at him. "Maybe if you talk to her she'll feel better."

Jeff nodded, praying he got the chance. "I think I'm the reason she's sad. I hurt her feelings and said some things I didn't mean."

"Can't you say you're sorry?"

"She doesn't exactly want to talk to me right now. I was hoping you could help me."

The boy turned his serious blue-eyed gaze toward him, reminding him so much of Trevor. "How?"

"I care about her, Colin, a lot." He released a long

breath. "And I want to be more than just friends with your mom," he rushed out.

The boy didn't look at him. "You mean get married like Zach's mom and Brandon?"

Jeff tried to relax with the gentle sway of the horse. "Yeah, but I want you to know, I'm not taking your father's place. Trevor Guthrie was the best man I ever knew and I was honored to be his friend." Jeff smiled through his sadness. "He raised two fine children, too. I'd be lucky if you'd let me share your life."

The boy looked him in the eye. "You mean you love us?"

Jeff swallowed as the realization hit him. "Yeah, I do."

Colin looked down at his reins. "Before Dad died, he told me some things." Tears filled the boy's eyes. "He asked me never to forget him, and to take care of Mom and Emily."

Jeff nodded. That was a big job for a little boy.

"Dad said that if I needed help with anything, I could ask you."

"I wish I could have been around more," Jeff told him.

Colin shook his head. "Dad said your life was the army. Someone had to keep our country safe, and you were the best man for the job."

Jeff's throat tightened so he could barely speak. "I tried, but I've had regrets, too. I didn't make it home in time to see your dad before he died. I only hope you let me hang around to be there for you and your sister."

The boy thought for a while. "You think we could go back to Three Rock Ridge sometime?"

Jeff's chest swelled. "Sure. Anytime."

Colin finally smiled. "So how are you going to get Mom not to be mad at you, so you can marry her?"

Jeff couldn't help but grin. "That's exactly what I need your help with."

It was just before dusk by the time Lacey and Nora finished feeding forty hungry trail hands. They were tired, but at least they didn't have to worry about clean-up. Hank had taken care of that by hiring some college kids.

Of course, they still needed be up at 5:00 a.m. She and Nora would spend the night in the trailer so they could get ready for an early breakfast. She was enjoying every minute of the trip.

Nora stretched her arms over her head. "I'll miss having Brandon next to me, but not enough to sleep on the hard ground."

Lacey smiled. "Yeah, a single bunk with a mattress is sounding pretty good to me right now."

She glanced over the camp as night began to fall. The sound of the calves mooing and laughter around the campfire was peaceful. She caught a glimpse of Colin with Zach, and they even had Emily with them.

Off in the distance, she caught sight of three riders on horseback coming into camp. She wasn't surprised to see Hank, Chance and Wyatt. They were greeted with enthusiasm by everyone. After a few minutes, Hank wandered over to them and hugged them both.

"How's it going?"

Lacey shrugged. "No one's complained about the food."

"All I've heard was praise about your stew and home-made rolls. They enjoyed Nora's pies, too." He winked at his grandson's wife before she wandered away.

"Well, we're sticking with the basics, hoping to please everyone. Tomorrow night, we'll grill hamburgers and I'll make some baked beans."

Hank studied her a moment. "I was hoping you'd find some time to enjoy this trip. That's the reason I hired the helpers."

"I'm not overworked, Hank," she protested, knowing she'd stayed busy to avoid Jeff. "You're paying me to do a job."

"You still can have some fun," he insisted as the sound of a strumming guitar drew their attention. "Come on," Hank coaxed. "Let's go enjoy the music." He took Lacey's hand and pulled her over to the fire ring where she sat down on a log beside her kids.

She was caught off guard to see Jeff was the one who was playing, and then she recalled years back when both Trevor and Jeff had attempted to learn the instrument.

It wasn't long before the group threw out song requests. The first was "Home on the Range," and another, "Yellow Rose of Texas." Jeff really got the crowd going as he then went into a Garth Brooks favorite and everyone broke into applause and cheers.

Once the group quieted, Jeff began to strum again, quietly. The few women in the group sighed when Jeff began singing a George Strait ballad, "The Man in Love with You."

Lacey glanced away. She didn't need this. She didn't want this from him. Yet she quickly got lost in the words.

Jeff had never been the kind of man to draw attention, but he had everyone's now, including hers. Finally he looked at her, and his eyes told her his feelings as he sang the last note.

Silence fell over the group as their gaze met momentarily. Her heart drummed against her chest, wondering if everyone could hear. Then the spell was broken as someone called out another song title.

Jeff began to play and she did the cowardly thing: got up and walked away.

"I never said it would be easy," Brandon conceded after the group broke up.

Jeff shook his head. "It was a crazy idea."

"Men do crazy things for the women they love."

Jeff swung around to see his dad standing behind him.

"The important thing is, son, keep trying." The older man raised an eyebrow. "I can't tell you how many times I could have cut my losses and walked away from your mom, but love kept me coming back."

"Yeah, but this is different from you and Mom."

"That might be, but I'd say you have an advantage over me. It's said people who've been in happy marriages are more willing to marry again." Wyatt shrugged. "Of course, if you feel you couldn't be a good husband to Lacey or a father to her kids…"

Jeff really didn't know, and yet… "I want the chance to try."

"All I can say is don't let it slip away," his father advised.

The next morning, Lacey felt disappointed when Jeff didn't come through the chow line at breakfast. Instead he sent Brandon because he was too busy.

"Well, I can be busy, too," she murmured while loading up the trailer to move to the next location. Already bored, Emily had left earlier when her best friend Megan and her mother had picked her up for a sleepover.

Lacey now had time to go home for a quick shower and a change of clothes before she was due at the next location for lunch. She climbed into the truck and watched as the last of the riders and cattle moved on down the trail. All but one lone cowboy.

Jeff had hung back. With everyone out of camp, he checked to see nothing was left behind, then kicked dirt over the cool campfire before he climbed on his mount. Surprisingly, he did it with ease as he swung his leg over the back of the horse. He sat straight in the saddle and took control of the animal, in spite of the fact he hadn't ridden for years and was missing part of a leg. Lacey's stomach tightened as she remembered their night together. They were good and bad memories at the same time.

"He's one of those men who are hard to get off your mind."

Lacey turned to see that Nora had climbed into the cab, catching her in the act of staring. "I've always cared about Jeff, he was my husband's best friend." She rushed on. "We were all friends back then."

Nora raised a hand. "That's good. Friends, then lovers."

Lacey was a little shocked at her blunt assessment. "That's the problem, we stepped over that line twice, and I think the baggage we both have ruined everything."

Nora frowned. "You can't tell me you two didn't sizzle."

They had. Even the first time when they'd been practically teenagers. Her stomach did a flip remembering their lovemaking the second time. Even better. "That doesn't automatically say we're meant for each other." At least Jeff didn't think so, Lacey thought as she started the engine and drove over the uneven terrain.

That didn't stop Nora. "Look, Lacey, I saw the condition of Jeff's leg at the hospital. He's a lucky man that he healed so quickly. And he's accomplished a lot so far." She motioned toward the rider and herd. "I'm not an expert on amputees, but he's probably loaded down with insecurities, especially when it comes to being able to please a woman. To feel like a whole man."

Lacey couldn't stop the rush of memories of their night together, or the blush.

Nora smiled. "He's just like all the other proud and stubborn Randells. Think about this, Lacey. Is the man worth another chance?"

By the second day of the cattle drive, Jeff's body had begun to feel the effects of his hours in the saddle. It was a good thing they'd arrived at camp, and so far there'd been no mishaps with any of the riders. They'd completed a count on the herd and discovered six cows missing. He sent out three of the experienced ranch hands, and within an hour they'd rounded up the steers.

He wasn't about to leave anyone behind, man, woman or bovine, even if he had to go search on his own. Maybe that would get his mind off Lacey. Yeah, right. It didn't seem to be working.

He rode around the herd that had settled down for the night. Thanks to the recent rains, they had full stock water troughs and plenty of summer grass to keep them happy. He glanced back toward camp and saw smoke coming from the grills. It was their last night on the trail, and they were going to have steak for supper.

The group of men and the few women deserved it. They'd worked hard. There wasn't a city slicker in the bunch, which made his job easier. Although he did miss not having a shower, a shave and good sleep for three days. Most of all he missed talking with Lacey. Yet, he couldn't state his case until they were off the cattle drive. Once home, he needed to make plans. He couldn't go to Lacey and ask her to share his life if he didn't have anything to offer her and the kids. He had to talk with Jay to see if he was serious about leasing the land.

He wanted to be more than just Lacey's business partner.

Jeff walked his gelding back into camp and climbed off. He was hungry, but first he had to check out the area. They had to make sure the bush was cleared so there wouldn't be any accidents or mishaps.

He caught Colin walking toward one of the portable outhouses for the guests. He tensed, knowing that cool structures were a perfect spot for creatures to get out of the heat.

Jeff stopped one of the ranch hands. "Have you swept the camp for snakes?"

The kid shrugged. "That's Marty's job today."

Jeff didn't wait to track Marty down. He took off for the outhouse just as Colin pulled open the door. The second he saw the kid freeze, he slowed his pace, hearing the rattling sound loud and clear.

"Don't move, Colin," he instructed in a low voice.

He knew that, as a Texan, Trevor would have taught his son about snakes.

"Jeff..." the boy managed.

"I'm right here, son." Jeff stepped a little closer to get a better look. Not good, the snake was cornered, and passing Colin was his only way out. Jeff couldn't tell how long the snake was, so he couldn't judge the striking distance.

Jeff felt someone behind him. Brandon.

"Do you have your gun with you?" Jeff asked, not moving.

"I grabbed your shotgun."

The idea didn't sound as good as he first thought. "Better not take the chance, I could miss. The best bet is to slam the door closed before the snake can strike."

"Tell me what to do," Brandon asked.

Jeff motioned for his cousin to go to the side of the outhouse door. Then Jeff slowly moved into position to get the boy to safety. With a nod, Brandon threw himself against the metal door and it slammed shut with a bang. At the same time Jeff pushed Colin to the ground, landing on top of the boy.

With the door safely closed, Jeff rolled over, feeling his bad leg hit the hard ground at a funny angle. But his first concern was the boy. He rose up. "You okay, son? The snake didn't get you?"

Colin managed to shake his head, fighting tears. "I'm okay."

"Good." Jeff rolled over onto his back and sat up. Rolling up his pant leg, he exposed his prosthesis while he shifted the rubber boot back into place over his knee, and then tugged his jeans back down.

Colin was watching him. "Did you get hurt?"

Jeff smiled wryly as he put his hat back on. "No, I just zigged when I should have zagged." He got to his feet as Lacey came running toward them. "Go to your mom, Colin." He gave the boy a shove and turned back to Brandon.

Grinning, his cousin tossed Jeff the shotgun. "Want to impress your girl?"

"You're real funny," he said, then took aim. "Ready," he called and Brandon opened the door. Within seconds the snake was history and with the help of a knife, it became a trophy. That brought several of the group to see what was going on. After a few slaps on the back to both Brandon and Jeff, everyone wandered back to camp.

Jeff was headed there himself when he heard his name called. He turned, knowing it was Lacey.

"Jeff, thank you. If you hadn't been there, Colin could have been bitten." Tears welled in her eyes. "I don't know what I would have done—"

He reached out and pulled her into his arms, loving the feel of her softness against him. "Ah, Lacey, don't. Don't play the what-if game. Colin's fine now. And I think he'll remember to check for snakes from now on." He searched her face, hungry for the sight of her. He'd missed her so much. It would be so easy to lean down and taste her sweet mouth. "You be careful, too."

She nodded, but didn't move. "I will." She swallowed and he could see the rapid pulse in her neck. "I guess I should go start supper." She gave him a half smile. "You've earned the biggest steak."

She went to leave, then stopped. Before he knew her plans, she leaned in and kissed his cheek. She paused as her gaze locked with his. "Thanks again, Jeff." She ran off.

Suddenly he broke into a big grin. "Just wait until we get back, Lacey Guthrie," he breathed. "I'm coming for you. This time I'm not letting you get away with a kiss on the cheek, and I'm definitely not letting you go."

CHAPTER THIRTEEN

THE next day around noon, they arrived at their destination, the Circle B Ranch. All steers and wranglers were accounted for. Jeff rose up in the saddle from about fifty yards out and spotted his dad, Uncle Cade and Uncle Chance waiting at the pens ready to separate the herd, the mamas from their calves.

There were more ranch hands to take over so the guests could go to their quarters, clean up and rest for the celebration later, although some of them wanted the full experience and planned to stay and help with the branding.

Jeff was going to pass this time. His job as trail boss was completed and he was headed to the cabin. After three nights on the hard ground, his single bunk looked pretty good to him. He planned to come back here tonight, and if he was lucky he'd have a date.

After he'd taken care of his horse, he walked over to the food trailer and Lacey. Colin was the first to see him.

"Hi, Jeff," the boy called.

Jeff tugged on the boy's hat. "Hi, Colin. You did a great job on the drive. Your dad would have been proud."

The kid's face lit up. "Thanks. It was fun, but I think I like working with horses better."

Jeff leaned forward. "So do I."

They both laughed as Emily joined in. "Mom said when I get older I can ride with the herd like Colin did."

Jeff couldn't resist the little girl and lifted her into his arms. "Well, you let me know when that is, and I'll help you practice herding cows."

Her blue eyes widened as she looked over her shoulder. "Mom, Jeff's going to teach me."

Lacey stopped her chores. "That's nice, Em. But right now you need to gather your things from the truck so we can go home."

"You'd better get busy." He set the girl down and the two kids took off.

Finally alone with Lacey, he turned to her. "Are you coming to the party later?"

Lacey shook her head. "I haven't worked Fancy in days."

"Will's been doing a pretty good job with the filly. Of course, he's not you, but Fancy seems to like him."

"Thank you both for handling things while I was away. That's the reason I need to stay home tonight."

Jeff wasn't going to let it go. "How about I come by and help you? The two of us can get it done faster and you can rest. You worked hard during the drive and deserve to have some fun."

Lacey didn't need to spend any more time with the man. "You don't have to do this, Jeff." She glanced away. "We made a mistake that night, and somehow we need to move past it and go on."

"Is that what you want? Just to forget everything?"

She could never do that. God help her, he would always have a piece of her heart. "It's for the best."

She just needed a way to stop loving him, to get things back to there being just business between them.

"We're not going to the party," Lacey said to her son hours later after they'd finished chores. "We're all tired from the trip and we need to spend a quiet night at home."

"But you've got to go, Mom. Jeff will be there. I know Mr. Hank will want to thank you, too."

"I'm sure he'll understand why I can't make it tonight. Besides, you kids start back to school tomorrow."

"We can go, too. Zach's going with his parents."

"Zach is a Randell. They're family."

Colin looked agitated. "We can be Randells, too, if you'd just go."

Lacey's head shot up to look at her son. "Colin, why would you say that?"

"Because Jeff told me—" He stopped. "Oh, never mind." He started out of the room.

"Colin Trevor Guthrie, you come back here."

"Oh, boy, you're in trouble," Emily whispered as her brother marched past her and stood in front of his mother.

"Please explain to me what you meant by that."

The boy released a long breath. "Jeff told me he wants to win you back."

She raised her hand. "Jeff talked to you about this?"

"Yeah, he asked me how I felt about him wanting to marry you."

Emily squealed and Lacey was speechless. Jeff wanted to marry her!

The boy went on to say, "He said he wouldn't take our daddy's place, but wanted to know if I'd mind if he helped raise us and married you."

Emily marched up to them. "Hey, he didn't ask *me*."

Colin glared at his sister. "Don't you want Jeff to be our new dad?"

She nodded. "Oh, Mom, please say yes. Jeff tells me stories about Daddy. He reads to me and he even kissed my dolly goodnight. I want him to be my new daddy so you're not sad anymore."

Lacey fought her rising hope. "Oh, honey, I'm not sad, I have you and Colin."

"Is it because Jeff doesn't have a leg?" Colin asked.

Lacey gasped. "Of course not. That doesn't matter to me." She looked back and forth between her kids. "What about your dad?"

"Dad told me Jeff was like a brother to him," Colin said. "Remember how he always talked about him?" Her son studied her. "Do you love Jeff?"

Her kids' gazes were leveled on her, waiting for an answer. "I loved your dad. You know that, don't you?"

They both nodded. "Can't you love Jeff, too?" Colin added.

"Yeah, Mom," Emily confirmed. "So put on a pretty dress and go to the party and tell him." She smiled. "Just like Beauty and the Beast, you can dance with him."

Colin groaned at his sister's fairytale reference, but didn't say anything.

Lacey felt her own excitement building. Her heart pounded with hope and fear as she looked at her children. "Kids, I might need to go to the party by myself."

Music played in the background as Jeff walked along the patio. He took another drink of water. He didn't want anything clouding his thoughts or senses.

He watched as couples two-stepped around the makeshift dance floor. Most of them were Randells, and none of the women were Lacey. He wasn't sure she would even show up, and his hopes were fading that he could say all the right things to finally win her over.

"Jeff?"

Hearing Lacey's voice, Jeff turned so quickly that he stumbled a little, reminding himself of his limitations. But once he saw her, he wasn't backing away.

He smiled. "You made it."

She nodded. "I found a sitter at the last minute."

"I'm glad." He looked over the woman he usually saw in jeans and T-shirts. Tonight she had on a long white gauzy skirt with a turquoise Indian print blouse which exposed her delicate shoulders, and a chain belt hugged her small waist. "Can I get you something to drink?"

"Thank you, maybe later. You could ask me to dance."

He swallowed. "I'm not sure I can keep up."

The music ended and a soft ballad replaced the quick beat. She took him by the hand and led him away from the crowded patio to the garden. She stepped onto the manicured lawn. "This looks like a good spot to practice."

Jeff didn't hesitate to draw her into his arms. The top of her head rested against his chin. With a love song in the background, his arms tightened and he pulled her against him so her breasts were pressed to his chest. She fitted perfectly. He couldn't speak, too afraid to break the spell between them.

About halfway through the song, Lacey pulled back and looked up at him. "I missed you when I was in Florida."

"I've missed you, too. Since the second you left the cabin that morning." His eyes searched her face. "Please believe me when I say I regret all the stupid things I said to you. It wasn't you, it was my insecurities talking." He stopped as the moonlight played across her face. "You're so beautiful."

"Keep talking. It sounds good so far."

He stopped moving. "I don't exactly feel like talking right now."

Jeff pulled Lacey back into his arms, then lowered his mouth to hers. At first he tried to go slow, but she tempted him so the kiss turned hungry and sparks went off. By the time he lifted his head they were both breathless.

"Oh, Lace. As much as I like where this is headed, this isn't the place. And there's too much I want to say to you." He wanted more than just a few stolen nights. He had to let her know he wanted them to truly be partners, in every way. "Okay, can we at least take this somewhere more private?"

Lacey felt as giddy as a teenager. At first, she'd thought she was crazy to get talked into this, but she couldn't deny her feelings for Jeff any longer. "Just to talk?"

"We definitely need to begin there," he said. "Because I want this to be a beginning for us, Lacey. I want more than a business partnership."

Her spirits quickly lifted. "I want that, too."

Jeff's mouth spread into a sexy grin. "Hold that thought. I need to tell Brandon I'm leaving." He grabbed her hand and walked her back to the edge of the patio. "I'll be right back." He gave her one last kiss and hurried off.

Lacey couldn't stop smiling as she watched several of the guests dancing. One of them was Jay Randell, busy talking with several young girls. He spotted her and waved, then came over to her. "Hey, Lacey, how about a dance?"

She smiled. "Sorry, all my dances are taken tonight."

Jay raised an eyebrow. "So Jeff finally won you over."

She nodded. Did everyone know what had been going on between them? "We're working on things."

"That's more good news to make my day. My loan was approved, so if you're agreeable we can go ahead and discuss the land lease."

Lacey frowned. "What are you talking about?"

"I guess Jeff hasn't told you about my offer to lease the acreage up by the cabin."

Lacey shook her head and remained calm.

"Hey, I bet he's planning to surprise you."

It hadn't taken Jeff long to find Brandon. After hearing Jeff's explanation of his early departure, his cousin gave his blessing, along with a key to a cabin in Mustang Valley.

"You're going to need help to convince her you're the man for her," he teased, then grew serious. "Tell her what's in your heart, Jeff. It'll work out."

Jeff went to find Lacey. He saw her standing with Jay and felt a pang of jealousy at the sight of his cousin talking to his girl. When he arrived, she wasn't smiling any longer.

"Sorry I took so long," he said, but Lacey didn't seem happy to see him.

"Guess what, Jeff?" she began. "Jay's been telling me an interesting story about a plan to lease my land."

Jeff glared at Jay. "It was just an idea he mentioned in passing. That's all."

Jay raised a hand in defense. "Hey, I didn't mean to cause trouble," he said, and was wise enough to make a quick departure. "I'd better go."

Lacey turned and started toward the parking area. Jeff caught up with her at her truck. At least they could talk privately. "I thought we were going to talk, Lace."

"Seems as if you've already discussed things with Jay, so you don't need me. You men are all alike." She didn't need to bring up Trevor's name, because they both knew who she was referring to.

"I know you think I went behind your back, but I didn't," he denied. "It was an idea Jay threw out a few weeks ago. I didn't know he was even serious until today."

"I still wanted a say in it."

He straightened, feeling anger building. "Then you shouldn't have run off to Florida." It had really hurt that she hadn't called him. "Business partners don't just walk away from one another."

"Look who's talking about running off! You're pretty good at it, too. Ten years ago you couldn't get away from me fast enough."

He didn't look away. "It was for the best. You and Trevor got back together."

She brushed her pretty blond hair off her shoulders. "So that's what you told yourself to make it all right? What about me? You gave no thought to *my* feelings. Did you think I made love to you to make Trevor jealous?"

"Of course not." He took a step closer and she backed away. "I cared about you then and I care about you now."

She hugged herself. "How can I believe that when

you never contacted me? To find out if I was okay." Angry tears welled in her eyes. "I wasn't, Jeff. I wasn't okay. I was pregnant."

A baby. Jeff felt the shock down to the pit of his stomach. "Oh, God." He reached for her and gripped her arms. "You were pregnant? Why didn't you tell me?"

"You'd already left for the army." She brushed away a tear. "You deserved to know, but before I convinced myself to write you, I'd miscarried."

The pain hurt so badly, he couldn't concentrate on her words. Lacey had been pregnant. With his child. "You still should have told me."

"Why? What would you have done? Offered to marry me?"

In a heartbeat. "Yes, I'd have married you."

She stiffened. "Funny, you didn't seem to want to be anywhere near me back then."

"I thought I was doing the right thing. You were Trevor's girl."

Another tear slid down her cheek. "That afternoon, I thought I was Jeff's girl." She wiped away the tears. "But I learnt fast what I meant to you."

He'd thought he'd been doing the right thing by leaving. "Did Trevor know about us? About the baby?"

She shook her head. "No. I couldn't hurt him. He was such a good friend. And he loved me enough to still want to marry me."

Totally stunned by her revelation, Jeff could only stand there as Lacey walked away without a backward glance.

Hours later, Jeff still hurt.

It was after midnight when he arrived back at the cabin. He'd been driving around, going over and over what Lacey had said to him. Her words had felt like a kick in his gut. They hurt worse than the bullet that had shattered his leg. She couldn't have been any plainer than that, taking away the last of his hopes to win her back.

He didn't blame Lacey. He'd walked away from her twice.

He went into the cabin and lit the lantern, then opened the windows to try and cool the place as Lonesome came to greet him.

Jeff sat down at the table and leaned forward to pet the dog. "Oh, buddy, I've messed everything up, when all I wanted to do was help her out. Instead I got too involved and ended up falling in love with her all over again." He knew that was a lie before the words came out of his mouth. He'd *always* loved her.

The thought of her being all alone and pregnant just about killed him. Back then he'd been so young and stupid. He should have known there'd been a chance it could happen. But he hadn't thought about that. All he'd wanted was to get out of town, to forget that she belonged to another man. His best friend.

He went to get a bottle of water and noticed Trevor's journal on the counter. He picked it up and carried it back to the table. "Hey, friend, I'm in trouble now." He closed his eyes momentarily, not knowing if he wanted to read more, and knowing he'd let his friend down, too. He needed some kind of closeness to the man who'd shared his childhood and loved the same woman. He opened the book to where he'd left off the other day.

It was dated a week before Trevor's death.

Jeff,

I don't know how much time I have left. Even the doctors can't say, only that they're still hoping for a miracle. I want to believe, too, but it's hard.

And it's hard to keep up a front with Colin and Emily. Damn, they're too young to be without their dad. My boy needs a man around to help him. My daughter is practically a baby.

So my friend, I'm calling in all favors. I need you to be there for them now. And Lacey. She acts tough, but she'll be hurting. I've been blessed these past ten years to have a wife who loves me and kids that make me so proud. The only thing is I won't be around to protect them and see how they turn out.

I know this is a big deal to ask of you, but I can't trust my family with anyone else. And you have all those Randell aunts, uncles and cousins, so share them with the Guthrie clan. We always said we were like brothers, now prove it. It shouldn't be a problem since they're all so easy to love.

Jeff felt tears on his cheeks and he wiped them away as he turned the page.

There's one last thing, friend. I've been lucky to have married Lacey and shared a life with her, but I know you always had a piece of her heart, too. Come home, Jeff. You need your family, and Lacey and the kids need you.

Goodbye, old friend,
Trevor

CHAPTER FOURTEEN

THE next day was like any other day, Lacey told herself. The kids had gone back to school that morning. Thank goodness, because they had too many questions about Jeff. Questions she couldn't answer.

Once they'd boarded the bus, she headed to the barn and to her job training Fancy. Something inside her made her hope that Jeff would come by. But why would he? Not after what had been said last night. All she could see was the pain etched on his face when he'd learned about the baby.

Was it possible to move on? To continue working together?

At lunch time, Lacey went to the house but wasn't hungry and ended up sitting on the porch, drinking iced tea. She closed her eyes, thinking back to only a year ago.

Trevor would have been with her. No, he hadn't had much time for her, not the last few years, anyway. It was clear that the ranch problems had taken a toll. Maybe if he had shared those troubles with her they would have been closer. Trevor had called it "protecting her." And he'd protected her far too often. It had left them nearly bankrupt and caused problems in their marriage.

How could she think that she could work with Jeff? It was even crazier to think she could start a relationship with him without the past intruding on them. Maybe she shouldn't have told him about the baby. But it had finally needed to come out.

That news had hurt him. She didn't need to relive the pain again, either. She had no choice but to move on without Jeff. Not that she'd ever had him, then or now.

She started to go inside when she spotted a truck coming down the road. Her breath caught as she recognized the dusty vehicle. Jeff's truck. It came to a stop next to the corral, and he climbed out.

She stood, her heart pounding against her ribs as he walked to the porch, but didn't come up the steps. "Hello, Lace."

She had to swallow before speaking. "Jeff. I didn't expect you today."

"For the moment we still have a partnership. There are some matters that need to be cleared up."

"I don't think we have anything else to say."

"That's where you're wrong, Lace." He came up the stairs as he pulled a manila envelope from his back pocket. "Here's the deed to the cabin property."

She backed away. "No, I can't take it, Jeff. I don't have the money to pay you back."

His gaze softened. "You still think that I bought the property for an investment? No. I bought it to help you and the kids, but yeah, to help myself, too. Truth is, I needed a purpose to get up out of bed, to want to work again. Buying your horses that day got me thinking about a future. So you see, Lacey, I needed you as much as you needed me." He paused, watching her. "It was always my intention to include you in all decisions. I never purposely tried to leave you out."

She swallowed hard, ashamed of her reaction to Jay's offer. "I know. I was surprised and angry."

He nodded. "But the important thing is I want you to know that I would never have left town if I'd known you were pregnant. I would have done anything for my child."

Lacey fought her emotions. "It's strange to talk about the baby after all this time. Afterwards, I just buried the memories and tried to move on and build a life with Trevor."

She looked at Jeff, seeing he was struggling with his emotions, too.

"Oh, God, Lace, I'm so sorry." When he reached for her, she went willingly into his tight embrace. After all these years they had the right to share their pain. "I'd give anything to have been here for you."

She let the tears fall. "I wish you had been here, too. So badly."

He drew back and looked at her. There were tears in his eyes. "How far along were you?"

"Eleven weeks. The doctor said it happens sometimes. It wasn't anyone's fault."

Her gaze met his, seeing his doubt. "We can't blame ourselves, Jeff."

"I need to know one thing… Did you want my baby?"

She nodded. "Yes, Jeff, I wanted our child." She glanced away. "I wanted a part of you."

He lowered his forehead to hers. "Oh, Lace, I want

that, too. I dreamt about it for years, but you were Trevor's wife."

"I'm not his wife any longer," she surprised herself by saying. "No more guilt about the past."

Jeff finally smiled. "You have no idea." He drew her back into his arms and lowered his mouth to hers in a searing kiss. She melted against him, reliving every dream she'd ever had about this man.

He broke off the kiss. "As much as I want to continue kissing you, and more, I need you to come with me first."

He tugged on her arm and she resisted. "I can't, the kids are due home from school."

He smiled. "I think there might be a Randell around to help with that." He pulled out his cell and punched in a number. "Nothing is going to stop us this time."

After getting Hank to come by to take care of the kids, Jeff drove Lacey to the cabin. It seemed like everything began there, and it was time to put it to rest before they started their beginning.

He leaned down and kissed her quickly, then got out and hurried around to her side to help her out of the truck.

"Come on, I want to show you something." They continued to walk past the cabin about a hundred yards. The late summer breeze was tolerable and there were mature oaks around the building site that promised shade from the heat.

He stopped on the edge of the ridge and looked out at the pasture. There were survey stakes in the ground to mark off the large house he'd planned to build here.

His pulse sped up seeing Lacey standing beside him

with the sun highlighting her hair. She was dressed in those slim-fitting jeans that made her legs look a mile long. She had her hands on her hips as if she were ready to take on the world. He loved all that attitude.

He was suddenly anxious, hoping she'd go for the idea. "I confess I kept this from you, but I wanted it to be a surprise."

She looked at him. "What is all this?"

"I want to build a home here." He paused and drew air in. He could smell her and he took a step back, trying to keep his head. He nearly stumbled. She reached for him and her touch was searing.

"So you're going to stay?"

He nodded. "I want to make a life here, Lace. It's something I've dreamed about for a long time. If I'd been honest with you that day in the cabin all those years ago, maybe you would have married *me.*" He gripped her hand. "It nearly killed me to leave, but I thought you loved Trevor, otherwise you couldn't have pried me away."

Lacey's green eyes stared back at him. "I know that now."

He forced a smile. "We can't go back, Lace, and question the decisions we made in the past. I thought I was doing the right thing."

"I know."

"I also want you to know I've always loved you, Lace. I've never stopped, and never will. I'm not talking about friendship. It's not enough after kissing you, making love to you," he breathed. "So, I'm asking you to give this gimpy ex-soldier another chance."

Her gaze searched his face as he tried to control his excitement. "Hey, I happen to love this gimpy ex-solder!"

He grinned. "You don't know how happy that makes me, because I happen to love this talented horse trainer. Her beauty, her kindness and how she fills out a pair of jeans." He kissed her again and again, feeling his body stirring. With a groan, he tore his mouth away and rested his head against her forehead. "I love you, Lace."

Tears rushed from her eyes. "Oh, Jeff, I love you, too."

He shivered at the words he'd always longed to hear. "The important thing is we found each other. And I'm not planning on losing you again."

"I don't want to forget the past, either."

"Of course not," he said. "There are too many good parts, and we can't forget Trevor. We both loved him." Jeff thought back to the journal. He hadn't wanted to bring it up today, but like everything else from now on he would share it with Lacey as soon as he could. This moment was theirs. Alone.

He reached for her hands, because he had to touch her. "Today is our beginning, Lace. I want it to be our start together. That's why I want this house for us, and the kids, too." He stopped and drew a calming breath, trying to find just the right words. "Funny, I've thought about this moment so many times…"

Lacey squeezed his hands. "Just say what's in your heart, Jeff. That's all I need to hear."

He nodded. "I need to do this right." He slowly got down on one knee. "You've always had my heart, Lacey Guthrie. I want to build a life together with Colin and Emily, and maybe another child, too. Will you marry me?"

A tear ran down her cheek. "Oh, yes, Jeff. Yes! I'll marry you." She pulled him up and went into his arms as his mouth took hers in a hungry kiss that only made him want her more.

Finally it was Lacey who broke off the kiss. "Oh, Colin and Emily."

"Granddad Hank can handle them, and we'll tell them later." He knew he already had a couple of allies. He started to tug her toward the cabin. "Right now, I want their mother to myself for a little while." He stopped and looked at her. "I know it will never replace the child we lost, but I want another baby with you."

She smiled and touched his face. "Oh, Jeff, I want to have your baby," she said softly. "You'd be a great dad, and you've already won Colin and Emily over."

He paused and his throat worked hard. She trusted him enough to share her kids with him. "You're sure the kids will be okay with us getting married?"

With a nod, she moved closer and kissed him sweetly. "And so is their mother."

Her trust meant everything to him. He pulled her to his side. "I still have Brandon's key to the cabin in Mustang Valley. I'll call Hank and see if he can play granddad until bedtime."

"Sounds like a good idea," Lacey agreed. "But I think we should be home in time to tuck them into bed. And after that, their mother's going to need your full attention."

"I like the way you think." They walked toward his truck. "Wait until later. I've got some more surprises for you."

Jeff glanced back at the cabin, knowing that he and Lacey had a lot more to talk about, to forgive, to share and to plan, but tonight it was for just them.

And all the good memories they were going to make. They were going to get their chance at a future. Together.

EPILOGUE

NEARLY a year later, Jeff looked up at the completed two-story, stone and cedar structure. Large oak trees framed the new Gentry home, and the rolling hillside made a perfect backdrop to complete the picture.

His heart swelled with love and pride, remembering the day six months ago when he'd married Lacey. They'd waited until after the one-year anniversary of Trevor's death before they became a true family.

He still had trouble believing he'd won Lacey's heart. Not too long ago he'd been a lonely soldier who couldn't fit in. Now he was a husband and father to a couple of great kids, living in a new house, getting a new beginning.

They'd only moved into the house two months ago, and were barely unpacked. But they were home. It was the Gentry home.

Will Jensen worked full-time now and lived in the apartment over the barn. Jay was renting the main house. He'd wanted to be closer to his herd.

Lacey went along with it, knowing the Guthrie house belonged to Colin and Emily, as did the ranch. All Jeff and Lacey owned was the section of land around the cabin. It was enough to eventually build a covered arena and barn closer to the house. That was further in the future.

Right now they were comfortable having Will help with the training. And they'd already welcomed the newest addition to the family, a colt from Bonnie and Ace, named Trevor's Pride. They wanted the kids to know their father lived on through the horses he loved.

Jeff thought of his friend a lot. He'd always miss him, but every day he got to see Colin looking so much like his father. Jeff would do everything to keep that memory alive.

He'd also shared Trevor's journal with Lacey. They'd laughed and cried together, cherishing their happy childhood, the years of friendship that they'd never forget.

Jeff found he loved working with horses, too. Maybe because he had the best partner—not only in the business but in life. He smiled. Yeah, he was one lucky guy.

"Hey, soldier, you looking for someone?"

He turned to see his wife coming toward him. She looked beautiful first thing in the morning, her sunny blond hair pulled away from her pretty face, those green eyes that smoldered when he loved her. He drew a breath as his gaze moved on to the worn jeans and fitted shirt. She was a pure Texas country girl. And she was his.

"I think I found her," he said and greeted her with a kiss that lingered awhile.

Lacey had never been so happy and she couldn't wait to share the reason with Jeff. "I like that greeting."

"There's always more where that came from," he assured her. "You heading over to the barn?"

"No, Will can handle things for a few hours."

Today wasn't about breeding or training. She had other plans for her husband. "You and I are going to play hooky. The kids have a half day of school, so later we're going to meet Brandon and Nora and their brood at Mustang Valley."

He pulled her close. "So that gives us a few hours to kill." He raised an eyebrow. "Got any ideas?"

She laughed, trying to hide her nervousness. "First I'd like to talk to you." She took his hand and together they walked to the creek that ran behind their house, but she went nearer to the cabin. This had been where they'd fallen in love.

He sobered and waited for her to speak. With a shaky hand, she reached into her back pocket and pulled out the pregnancy test stick. "It's positive."

He looked down at it with a shocked expression.

She smiled, knowing they'd been planning a baby since they'd moved into the house. They just didn't expect it would happen so soon. "I'm pregnant."

"A baby? We're having a baby?"

She nodded. "I believe it happened the first night in our new bedroom, on that wonderful new mattress. Or maybe it was the next morning in our new double shower, or—"

Jeff finally came out of his shock and kissed his wife. When he tore his mouth away, he was breathless. "I love you, Lace." He closed his eyes, thanking God for this blessing. "I'm going to take care of you this time. Nothing's going to happen."

She touched his jaw. "I know you will, Jeff. And I'm going to be careful, too. I'm done riding for now."

"And you're not lifting anything heavy." He grasped her hands. "I wish I could help you more."

She smiled. "Okay, when the time comes, I'll let you handle the labor."

"I would if I could."

"Right, Mr. Tough Guy. You'd crumble in minutes."

"I probably would, but I'm going to be there with you, every moment." He broke out into a big grin. "Damn. We're going to have a baby." He pulled her into his arms and kissed her again and again.

"So you starting something, cowboy?" she asked. "Just remember we only have a few hours before the kids get home." She grinned. "So you'd better take me back to the house and see if we can be creative in another room."

"Sounds like a great way to celebrate."

Jeff glanced one last time at the cabin. It was time to move on. He turned back to his wife and together they walked toward their future. Being away had only made him appreciate everything he had, especially now, having his family around him. He was a Randell, after all. This was where he belonged, with the woman he'd always love.

He was home. For good.

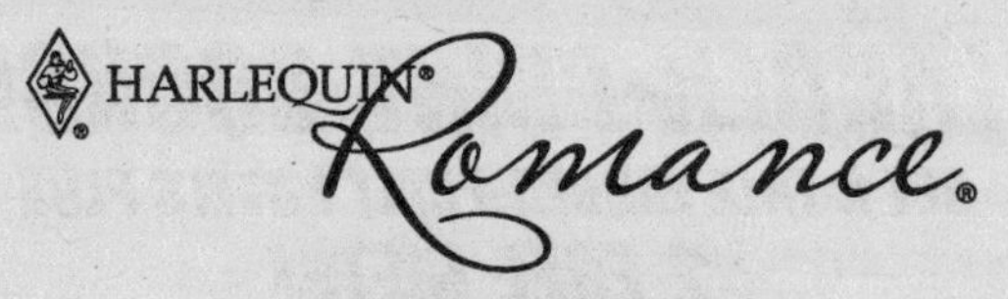

Coming Next Month

Available July 13, 2010

#4177 A WISH AND A WEDDING
Margaret Way and Melissa James

#4178 THE BRIDESMAID'S SECRET
Fiona Harper
The Brides of Bella Rosa

#4179 MAID FOR THE MILLIONAIRE
Susan Meier
Housekeepers Say I Do!

#4180 SOS: CONVENIENT HUSBAND REQUIRED
Liz Fielding

#4181 VEGAS PREGNANCY SURPRISE
Shirley Jump
Girls' Weekend in Vegas

#4182 WINNING A GROOM IN 10 DATES
Cara Colter
The Fun Factor

Introducing McFARLANE'S PERFECT BRIDE
by USA TODAY *bestselling author Christine Rimmer, from Silhouette Special Edition®.*

Entranced. Captivated. Enchanted.

Connor sat across the table from Tori Jones and couldn't help thinking that those words exactly described what effect the small-town schoolteacher had on him. He might as well stop trying to tell himself he wasn't interested. He was powerfully drawn to her.

Clearly, he should have dated more when he was younger.

There had been a couple of other women since Jennifer had walked out on him. But he had never been entranced. Or captivated. Or enchanted.

Until now.

He wanted her—*her,* Tori Jones, in particular. Not just someone suitably attractive and well-bred, as Jennifer had been. Not just someone sophisticated, sexually exciting and discreet, which pretty much described the two women he'd dated after his marriage crashed and burned.

It came to him that he...he *liked* this woman. And that was new to him. He liked her quick wit, her wisdom and her big heart. He liked the passion in her voice when she talked about things she believed in.

He liked *her.* And suddenly it mattered all out of proportion that she might like him, too.

Was he losing it? He couldn't help but wonder. Was he cracking under the strain—of the soured economy, the McFarlane House setbacks, his divorce, the scary changes in his son? Of the changes he'd decided he needed to make in his life and himself?

SSEEXP0710

Strangely, right then, on his first date with Tori Jones, he didn't care if he just might be going over the edge. He was having a great time—having *fun,* of all things—and he didn't want it to end.

Is Connor finally able to admit his feelings to Tori,
and are they reciprocated?
Find out in McFARLANE'S PERFECT BRIDE
by USA TODAY *bestselling author Christine Rimmer.*
Available July 2010,
only from Silhouette Special Edition®.

SSEEXP0710